This is a comedy about the things that go on in the hidden worlds inside our heads and all around us.

The other books in the series are *Paradise – A Divine Comedy* and *The Wheels of the World*. The Kindle or ebook version of *Paradise* is available free from Amazon and other internet bookshops.

For more, visit glennmyers.info

In the same series:
*Paradise — a divine comedy*

*The Wheels of the World*


… absolutely loved it. A hysterical surrealist take on what is out there after life on earth, or next to life on earth, or simultaneous with life on earth, or whatever. A story of Gods in kilts, crystal clear memories, and walls made of our pixelated fears. Delightful. (4 stars) Jeannette M. (Goodreads.com)

… Sometimes you want to hit the main character on the back of the head and tell him to stop being a wuss, but how would you react if you had to build a paradise controlled by some used-car-salesman-style gods? If you like quirky and surreal stories about the afterlife, then I would highly recommend *Paradise*. (4 stars, Katie Webb, Goodreads.com)

Superb rollercoaster of a story; loved every minute! (Phil Groom, book blogger)

So hilariously funny! I've already started reading the next one. I would highly recommend this to just about anyone. (Stewartc85 on Goodreads)

Myers is a great writer and his style is terrific… this was a great book (Martin Gibbs Amazon.com, Goodreads.)

What a great book! … a delightfully comic but definitely insightful look into the human psyche and soul … I loved every aspect of it. (4 stars, S Sutton, Amazon.com)


*


In an example of life following fiction, Glenn Myers was in a coma for a month shortly after writing the *Wheels of the World*. He hallucinated wildly in the two weeks it took to wake up. He thinks these hallucinations have now stopped and he made a full recovery.

# The Sump of Lost Dreams

**Glenn Myers**

**British Library Cataloguing in Publication Data**
A CIP catalogue for this book is available from the British Library
Printed by Lightning Source UK Ltd, Chapter House, Pitfield, Kiln Farm, Milton Keynes MK11 3LW UK.
Printed on paper from managed, sustainable forests, certified by the FSC (UK books) and the SFI (US books)

For Emma Harding, even though you're not quite big
enough yet

… Perhaps there walks a spirit
Close by, who pities me,—

A spirit who hears me tapping
The five-sensed cane of mind
Amid such unguessed glories—
That I am worse than blind.

Harry Kemp *Blind.*

with thanks to Arthur C Clarke who quoted the
poem, slightly incorrectly, in his book *Profiles of the
Future*.

# THIS MIGHT HELP

If you haven't read the earlier two books—and nobody's perfect—start here.

*

A prickly foreboding; an ache of desire; an insight flitting through the mind. These rise from a parallel dimension of spirits, souls, moods and memories: the heavenly places.

I know, because I work there.

This is one of the very few perks from having a head-on car-crash with an angry young female lawyer. Keziah and I suffered near-death experiences, each of us was catapulted into the heavens, each of us eventually got our lives back, and we now commute across dimensions between the earth and the heavens.

Apart from the fact that Keziah and I work together, our jobs are enormous fun. The heavens are a complicated, many-layered realm of evil spirits, admin centres, clouds of melancholy and fairground rides. They teem with spiritual life, some of it intelligent, some of it stupid, much of it dangerous.

The heavens are also busy with the traffic jam of human souls. This is because souls don't live inside bodies, despite what people think. Souls are too big and complex: quivering stacks of memories, ideas, opinions and fears. They are pulled through the heavenly places by spiritual beings known as pengubim (pengub is the singular) and steered by the inclination of our hearts.

So: souls are these big divots of landscape being towed through the heavens. Bodies? They'll be the meat, bone, wiring and pipework that lumbers about on earth. What links the two? Our spirit—the tiny, feisty true bit of us that constantly flits between the dimensions. One instant the spirit is inside the body; the next it's steering the soul through the heavens—depending on whether we are at that moment focusing on our outer or inner lives.

We who have had near-death experiences can detach our spirits from both body and soul and travel independently. So, our new career.

Souls can become gripped by compulsions or overrun with old memories. They can struggle through clouds of gloom and be sucked into a vortex of self-pity. Or they can be green and lush. Sometimes they are herded and milked by hungry spiritual beings; sometimes they are fertilized and pruned; sometimes watered by grace or beauty.

Keziah and I do what your friends do, if they are the interfering kinds of friends, or maybe what prayers do. We try to fix souls. She or he who fixes souls, fixes the world.

We are part of a heavenly team, called the Cambridge Area Network Soul Repair Team, to which someone, not I, gave the naff abbreviation the CANSORT.

We were recruited by two other humans who have also experienced near-deaths. One is Dr Corrie Bright, an extremely elderly academic who can slip out of her body whenever she wishes, in the knowledge that her carers on earth will think she's fallen into an old-lady doze.

The other is the former Old Testament prophet Jonah, who had his near-death moments in the belly of a fish and is buried deep under Mosul in Iraq. He has lived in the heavenly dimensions for many centuries, always working with world-leading cities. Since moving to Cambridge he has made it such a wellspring of genius that it's frankly embarrassing and people have noticed.

If you live in our noble city, you might have felt our labours on your soul: rolling an idea forward, dropping a hint, nudging a fresh thought into your consciousness. But probably not: most people are deaf most of the time and we are understaffed so we concentrate on either the most desperate or the most urgent.

But if you live in Cambridge and have ever been struck by a novel thought, especially if that thought was accompanied by a whispered argument in the background, hey, it may have been us.

Two further members complete our team. Stub is an evil spirit. He'll be the seven-foot-high ghoul whom you meet in the heavens wrapped in a coat and hat, pale as a heroin addict and red-eyed. He is trying to work his way back to favour with a God whom he believes in, fears and hates with equal measure. Finally the gorgeous Kirsty, bartender at the *Shepherd*

*Diner*, which is the restaurant and lido in the heavens that is our base. She is a gossiper, the class of beings who do all the cleaning and hospitality in the heavens and store all the knowledge.

Do not make patronizing remarks about her spending her days cooking, cleaning and transferring information. She is proud of her work, quite tall, and will likely injure you in creative ways.

The adventure you're about to read is mostly a story of two girlfriends and planning permission for a cafe.

Underneath these minor bumps in history's highway, though, were violent heavenly conflicts that sought to spread poison through our culture and destroy us and those we loved.

I'll leave you to decide whether we finished up wounded or healed, and whether we found a happy ending.

The heavens are too much to take in, so you use filters to simplify things. It helps to view souls as landscapes, and our human spirits and evil spirits as vaguely human forms. Because the heavens are a realm where metaphors have muscle, you can create things there just by thinking of them and ... you'll see the rest.

The food's good too.

# THE GRAND CENTRAL CENSER

The Grand Central Censer lurches through the high heavens as if wielded by a priest who is paid per swing. It is hemispherical, bronze, burnished, smoking and the size of Greater London. At the end of each swing, or sometimes just in its own sweet time, a huge glop of golden liquid slops out of the Censer and tumbles through the heavens. It thins into rain. Some of this rain lands on souls which either drink it in or sluice it off. The rest cascades down still further, to Vanity Fair where more souls mill around, queuing to go on the rides. If it isn't absorbed there, it tumbles deeper still towards Pandemonium where evil spirits shelter unsatisfactorily in poorly maintained buildings. It scalds them, and they curse the rain, or visit their Complaints Department.

The golden rain is undeserved kindness, as real and inexplicable as starlight.

# PRINCIPAL BEAN BREWER

The coffee machine in the disused crèche in the church of St Mary Magdalene in Cambridge steams and clanks in lonely glory atop a filing cabinet recently emptied of Sunday School lessons. It looks down on three scuffed desks and a lino-tiled floor.

Outside St Mary Magdalene—*Madge's* to its friends—Cambridge might be busy and bright with tourists, the colleges' carved stone lit by the sun. Inside, fan heaters fail to dispel eight centuries of Fenland chill and damp.

The coffee machine was the former principal bean-brewer in the deep-carpeted foyer of the venture capitalists Wood, Main and Bright. When Mark Bright cashed in his share and left the company, Wood and Main pressed the moody performer on him, eyeing instead a one-touch bean-to-cup dispenser, whose two-thousand-pound price tag theoretically meant perfect coffee even when made by Wood or Main.

I usually made the coffee in our makeshift office, dropping work for a few minutes to focus fully on the pressure gauge and the steamed-milk tube, and briefly fantasizing I was running a nuclear power station or piloting a voyage to Mars. I had discovered that Mark Bright, who often claimed to want a cappuccino but then forgot to drink it, and our colleague the Rev

Michael Collins, who watered himself only with fair trade tea from unbleached bags, were neither of them true believers.

This was not good. Mark—the venture capitalist—and Michael—the cleric—were about to be hit by a storm. Mark is unusual. Apart from being wealthy, tall, kind, stylish and self-effacing—and thus a little boring to girls in my view—he is one of those people whose actions resonate. Somehow, whatever Mark does echoes across communities and cultures. I don't know why this is. He pushes an idea forward, and the networks around him trill with excitement and fall into line.

The evil spirits know this. And now Mark was making his first punt since leaving Wood, Main and Bright. After much agonizing, he had formed a social enterprise, with his own money. His idea was to nurture local charities to national scale.

Rev Michael Collins ran such a charity. Twice a week he opened a free lunch-club and homelessness centre—the Oyster Café—in Madge's. With Mark's money and expertise, Michael wanted to turn this into a daily operation, in a building of its own, alongside office space for homelessness services. Michael was Mark's first client.

I was the information designer for both of them. This was my first job after my brief but catastrophic meeting with Keziah's Mini on the A428. I was enjoying working again, and the informality of our startup worked well given that my life was still speckled with medical appointments and ragged with incomplete healing.

If all came out right, what Michael built here, and what Mark then took to national scale, would start dismantling mechanisms of social injustice in the heavens.

The evil spirits, who had put a lot of effort into these mechanisms, were not happy.

In short: the time was coming and was now here when we needed good coffee.

*

I heard a brisk swishing up the stone stairs outside.

'Two steps backwards,' said Mark, as he pushed open the oak door, stooping slightly. In his early thirties, Mark had floppy dark hair and a pricey suit. Michael and I looked up. 'The planner said we would definitely need planning permission and he thought it would be turned down.'

'How did he contrive that?' Michael asked mildly. Bookish, in his sixties and with thinning hair, he gets to use words like 'contrive'.

Mark hung up his overcoat. 'I think he just took against the project. I could see him lining up in his head all the different ways to stop it. First you need planning permission because it's a change of use. Which it isn't. Then all the community will object because of the dodgy characters you're inviting in. Which depends how you go about it. Finally it's a prime site for housing. Which it definitely is.'

'Cappuccino?' I asked.

'I don't just need the diminutive. I need a whole monastery of Capuchin monks.'

Mark sat down at his empty desk. 'I saw our emails while I was waiting. Our application for their spare Section 106 money? The council have lost it. Probation were going to definitely get back yesterday about leasing an office but the person is off sick and it won't be until next week. DrinkClever have confirmed that our offer doesn't fit their current plans. Drugsense? See DrinkClever. Centre for counselling? Awaiting trustees' meeting. In two months.'

'Our surveyor rang while you were out,' said Michael. 'Most of the call was the sibilance of his indrawn breath and the whistles of his incredulity.'

'The dry rot,' said Mark wearily.

'More than he first thought.'

'How much?'

'His estimate alone was five thousand pounds.'

'I'm going in for the frothed milk,' I said. I clanked about, checked the temperature, pulled the lever. The coffee machine shook and spat.

'So brief summary,' said Mark. 'The Oyster Cafe. A pay-what-you-can restaurant and a network hub for the needy and destitute. On the one hand we have the offer of a building, the Strict and Particular Baptist Chapel ideally situated on Mill Road. We have a visionary CEO, respected cleric and pioneer of social justice initiatives, Rev Michael Collins.' He nodded at Michael. 'We also have Jamie on staff'—Mark nodded to me—'whom I am assured, mostly by him, is a talented communications professional.

'On the other hand. For our café and network hub for the homeless, we have just one taker for our office space, so it's hardly going to be a one-stop-shop. We have five thousand pounds of dry rot. And now we have the enthusiastic opposition of the Planning Department.'

'I don't know how to break this to you,' I said, 'but we're also out of chocolate sprinkles.'

'Added to the list,' muttered Mark.

'What do we do about the dry rot?' I asked.

Mark sighed. 'We can still cover the startup costs and recoup it later but it makes everything a bit tighter.'

'So what happens next?'

'Our architects have gone off to prepare proper plans. Council will have to respond in eight weeks.'

'Buys us some breathing space,' I said.

'I suppose.' Mark stared briefly at his empty desk.

'Your cappuccino,' I said.

Mark looked at it, which was all he mostly did with cappuccinos.

'Did you see Keziah last night?' I asked. Keziah's legal practice was our one confirmed client for the office space. Her speciality (on earth) was defending the truly lost in the Magistrates' Courts. She and Mark were also, as of not very long, dating.

'She fitted me in for noodles after work,' said Mark. 'We were seated by ten o'clock.'

'Where did you go?'

'The Japanese place with the uncomfortable benches.'

Mark looked in vain round his empty desk. He frowned at his coffee again. 'Not used to being held at arm's length,' he said.

'That's quite good for Keziah,' I replied.

'I wasn't meaning Keziah,' said Mark coldly. 'I was meaning everybody else.'

'Oops,' I said.

Mark looked at me. 'You and Keziah never did get on, did you?'

'No,' I said. 'We used to go out for coffee sometimes after we both got out of hospital. Since the crash was her fault I think she felt obliged. But for some reason I kept driving her nuts.'

'Odd,' said Mark.

'No accounting for people.'

This conversation about Keziah was at best a tango with the truth, but it wasn't absolutely a lie.

I saw Keziah later that night.

# HOT AND SOUR CASHEWS

Part of our heavenly job was inspecting each other's souls. When you work together in this business you need a certain transparency, hence the requirement to give each other a regular look-over.

It was not the favourite part of our week. Over the months, we have learnt not to comment much when being shown around.

Keziah phoned me on earth, as arranged, at 2:00am.

'You ready?'

'Eurrgh.' 2:00am is a particularly gruesome time to be woken up, your body cold, your brain powered down.

'See you up there.'

I watched the phone screen go dark, yawned, lay on my back, gently unhooked my spirit and with a barely a flicker of changing scenery, left my bedroom and arrived on my soul.

My spirit, like yours, is my pure essence and by convenient arrangement looks just like a version of me. My soul looks like an island landscape, being towed through the heavenly places by a pengub. At the front of my landscape is a cricket pitch. On the edge of the pitch is a pavilion. At the back of the pavilion, on the very edge of my soul, is the groundskeeper's room. It contains a wooden captain's chair that looks out of a window into the heavens. Here I sit—here my spirit sits—to steer my soul. This view resolved around me.

Metaphor, image, story and truth all swirl together in the heavens, so you can create real-looking things just by thinking about them. I conjured up a strong cup of tea in a vast white mug and positioned it on a little table just next to the ship's wheel, along with a couple of oat-and-honey confections half covered with milk chocolate.

Three thick strings extend from underneath the pavilion out to the pengub. A complicated mechanism enables me to tug the strings and steer the pengub by using a ship's wheel. I can spin left or right or pull up or push down and the willing pengub, whose name is Henry, will change direction for me.

I settled myself in the seat and took a sip of tea.

As is sometimes the case when I first wake up, I saw my soul was shrouded in mist which hung around it, growing faintly green. I could hear unearthly shrieks which I knew belonged to flying creatures like prehistoric reptiles who could suddenly appear in the fog and start jabbing my soul with their beaks.

I thought of the *Shepherd Diner* to which I was going with its warmth and light and good food and splashing lido.

'C'mon Henry,' I said. 'The *Diner*.'

The strings tightened and Henry pulled us skywards. We shook off the green fog, and emerged into the full light of the heavens, busy as a cityscape or a crowded aquarium.

Henry knew the way, which was basically *up* until you saw the *Diner's* navigation light. But I was still waking and it looked like my sleeping soul had drifted near a region of Vanity Fair that was a scrapyard of tatty but still potent rides. Several very old arguments rotated gently in the near distance, perfect for the just-waking soul to get sucked into while not yet thinking straight. I steered past a merry-go-round entitled *I should never…* and even though we were moving quite fast, it stirred up a memory in my soul. I should never have tried giving Lottie (my now ex-girlfriend) a reassuring caress after the tour guide turned off the lights in a cave to show us what total darkness is like. When they put the lights back on, I'd found myself stroking the bottom of a rather large man with lots of tattoos.

'C'mon Henry,' I said, 'up up up'.

We managed to dodge completely an octopus-like creature called *Embarrassing Memories of Adolescent Sexual Encounters*. Thankfully. And steered our way to somewhat clearer space.

We had a straightforward journey after that, apart from spending a few minutes being tugged sharply leftwards by a heavenly current evidently called *Pointless Political Arguments that I Rehearse Endlessly in my Head.*

The *Shepherd Diner and Lido* has vaguely Spanish architecture: whitewashed adobe walls and red roof-tiles. A building complex, it is pulled through the heavens by its own pengub. I noticed Keziah's little pengub swimming alongside it, a fish beside a whale. Keziah's soul, a delta-winged mountainous landscape, was being towed behind the *Diner.*

I parked, tied up, and unhitched. I do not know how intelligent pengubim are, but when they are together, they communicate in speech bubbles. I am told that they are all extroverts and refuel each other through mutual affection. 'Henry!' burbled the two pengubim when they saw the newcomer. 'Hello' signalled Henry, and then 'got a bit caught in a political drift down there'.

'Never mind,' flashed the big pengub, and then, 'Tell us some more stories about Jamie.'

I left them to it.

I stepped off my soul onto the *Diner*, which has a pavement cafe out front. Keziah was not there, so I walked through to the bar. That too was empty, until a being who presented as a tall, elegant New Zealand girl, effortlessly gorgeous in T-shirt and shorts, stepped out of the kitchen.

'Hello Kirsty,' I said, noting the waft of jasmine and coriander that had come through the door with her. 'That smells good.' Kirsty is a gossiper, the class of beings in the heavens who store all the information, and do most of the hospitality.

'For later. A drinkie,' she said, taking down a bottle and shaking lime juice into a glass. Then she filled the glass with soda from a tap.

'Can't I just … sample the food? Quality control?'

'No. Keziah's in the Lido with Mr Happy.'

Kirsty and Stub, gossiper and reformed evil spirit, did not get on.

'Mood?' I asked.

'His usual bubbly self. You know, I'm always saying, Stub, ease off the relentless optimism.'

'And the lawyer?'

'Thoughtful.'

'Nice change from homicidal.'

'Don't talk about Mark.'

'OK. Is it going badly?'

'No.'

'They've only been going out for a month!'

'I'm just saying,' said Kirsty. 'It's delicate. Leave it be.'

'Underneath the deceptively calm waters a dread monster lurks?'

'Something like that.'

'Those who foolishly throw down a hook into those waters are sucked into an emotional vortex beyond the edge of horror?'

'No. More like, just don't trample in with your muddy boots.'

'I think you underestimate me.'

'That would be a thing,' she said.

'Has Stub been somewhere?'

'Yes. And he has news.'

'What?'

'Grim, I expect. Sour and hot cashews,' she added, passing me a small bowl. 'Made by my own fairs. Don't eat too many.'

'Thank you.'

I carried my snack and drink through the wooden bar and then crossed a boardwalk with tropical plants on either side. By the pool, the tall evil spirit and the punk lawyer were facing each other at a table. Stub wore his usual mac and hat, shielding his scars from the rain. His face was in shadow under the rim of his hat, but red eyes gleamed.

Keziah was slight and pale in leather trousers and pink top and was shod with boots that looked good for denting heads. She wore shoulder length black hair and too much eyeliner. Her lips, which always pointed down, were grey.

'Hello both,' I said. 'You OK?' I asked Keziah.

She shrugged. 'You?'

'Yeah.'

'Good.'

'Good. Legal business still—'

'Busy.'
'Plenty of felons, desperadoes and low-life?'
'Yes.'

Conversational cupboard already nearly bare, and this was us being nice to each other.

'Did Mark say?' I asked Keziah. 'They insisted on planning permission for the chapel and hinted they'd decline it.'

'He sent me a text.'

'Not good.'

'No.'

I put the drinks and snack down.

'You're back,' I said to Stub. 'Where've you been?'

'Vanity Fair, sir.'

'Go on any of the rides?'

'No sir.'

'Not even the Vortex of Fear? I would have thought you couldn't resist swinging by.'

'No sir.'

'Or a quick skitter down the Slope of Hopeless Despair? You could whizz.'

'I do not find these matters a subject for levity, sir.'

'True wit is a rare flower, Stub. What were you doing?'

'I was eavesdropping for Dr Bright.'

'Find anything juicy?'

'I was explaining to Miss Mordant. Vanity Fair was rife with rumours. About Miss Mordant and you.'

'They're not true,' I said.

'And Mark Bright and Michael Collins.'

'And?'

'It seems you have been singled out for special attention. Apparently you are making a stir. In the heavens.'

'We are?'

'You are an irritation. An itch that needs to be scratched, sir.'

'Huh.'

'They have orders to neutralize you.'

'Neutralize.'

'Yessir. Have you heard of the Sump of Lost Dreams?'

'No.'

'It's the sewer system in Vanity Fair. Their idea, as I understand it, is to so break your hearts that you all end up there.'

'And then,' added Keziah, 'We spend the rest of our lives poisoning whatever we've built on earth.'

'The evil spirits would also get to feed on you, sir, which is an incentive for them.'

I took three cashews from my bowl, two sour and one hot this time, wondering momentarily what the odds of that were.

'Oh,' I said. 'Not good.'

I noticed my resolve was failing to harden and my eye was not piercing Stub with a determined look. I must have been away when they did fortitude at primary school. 'Can't we—'

'What?' asked Keziah.

'I don't know. Keep our heads down for a bit.'

She looked at me. Warmth and empathy did not fill her eyes.

'Until, you know, it washes over,' I went on.

'Washes over.'

'Yes.'

'Ease off the social justice until things wash over?'

'Yes.'

'Stop fighting for the poor until the situation cools off?'

'Possibly.'

'No.'

I took some more nuts. 'I don't want a fight.'

'They didn't ask,' said Keziah.

'You don't mind a fight.'

'Of course I mind!'

'But it's outside my skill set!'

'Oh well I'll just phone up and cancel, shall I?'

I looked at her. 'What are we supposed to do?'

Stub coughed. 'If I may say so, sir. Jonah and Dr Bright have arranged a strategy meeting for a little later in the night. Our lady bartender is cooking a meal for us. In the meantime, sir, you and Miss Mordant are urged to keep an especially a careful eye on each other's souls.'

'That's depressing,' I said.

'So let's get it over with,' said Keziah. 'Have you finished those cashews?'

'Does it matter?'

I let her lead the way out of the *Lido* and toward my soul. We left Stub to brood moodily, which he always did rather well.

# LOTTIE-LAND

'See,' I said to Keziah, 'I think the re-landscaping is going really well. What you are seeing is not the old Jamie who hides from bad memories or people he doesn't like.

'This isn't the sad Jamie who burrows himself among his good memories and avoids issues.

'This is the Jamie who is coming to terms with everything on his soul, the upgraded, empathetic, sensitive and reasonable Jamie.

'I point this out just in case you didn't notice.'

We'd climbed up from my cricket pitch onto a little hill and were considering the depths of my soul. Doing this with Keziah at your shoulder was still unnerving, but I was determinedly breezy. 'Feel free to take notes,' I said, 'on how to make peace with yourself.'

Annoyance was steaming off Keziah like she was wet washing in the sunshine.

'What I'm trying to do,' I said, a shade more genuinely, 'is stop my soul being such a wasteland and make it more like a garden.

'When I come across a bad memory I try to reason with it and we settle things with a handshake. Or sometimes it just stumps off. Either way that's a win.'

We walked on through my soul. We hadn't seen anything too alarming. All souls get landed on by small flying spiritual animals who come to snack on the soul's fruit. Could some of them be reporting back to more powerful spiritual beings? Presumably they could.

A fine rain was falling even this far from the Golden Censer and of course we both knew that the real reason my soul was changing was that I was no longer sluicing this rain off. I was letting it fall into my soul and produce its fruit.

We were in the hills on my soul, overlooking the valley where I kept most of my memories.

'What's that wall?' Keziah asked, pointing to a feature that I'd hoped was hidden behind a fold in a hill.

'That—that would be a … wall,' I said.

She tramped towards it. 'I haven't seen it before. What's on the other side?'

'Behind that? Oh, you know. More soul,' I said.

'It's huge.'

'A mere administrative division,' I said.

She'd reached it by now. It was brick and several feet higher than either of us. It stretched away and bent out of sight in either direction.

'Is that you, Jamie?'

We both heard the voice from the far side of the wall.

'Hello Lottie.'

'It's not like it's a surprise,' said the voice. 'Who else did you expect to find?'

'Fair point. I was just thinking how nice it was to hear your voice,' I added hopefully.

'I'm looking for a gate.'

'Why?'

'That would be because I want to leave.'

'How can you leave?' I asked. 'You are *my memory*. This is *my soul*.' It was not a wise question.

'I, Jamie, am an authentic memory. I am surrounded by lots of made-up memories. I no longer feel at home. That is why I wish to leave.'

'That's exactly the point!' I insisted. 'You're a real memory. You're…'

'Superfluous,' she finished. 'You seem to have plenty to keep you entertained here without me.'

Keziah's body language to my side suggested she may be smiling to herself.

'Ah,' continued Lottie, from over the wall. 'I see something.'

Keziah and I spotted it too, a wooden door in the brickwork not far away.

As we approached, its latch opened, and a thin tall girl with a small face and curly yellow hair walked out.

She was adjusting her skirt and glasses, and her hair looked a bit ruffled.

'Lottie!' I said brightly. 'You've met Keziah. She's a lawyer. If ever you're drunk and disorderly in a public space she's the hottest stuff.'

Lottie smiled at her.

'And Keziah, this a real memory of the actual Lottie.'

'And there aren't many of us,' said Lottie, to Keziah, finishing adjusting her clothes and smoothing her hair.

'Oh, I don't know,' I put in.

'And what doesn't seem to be in your collection of memories is my marriage to Umberto. To which, I seem to remember, you came as a guest.'

'Odd,' I said. 'Probably there somewhere if you hunt.'

'All I could see was fiction spreading as far as the eye could see. Bucolic scenes of Jamies and Lotties in a hayloft or a wheatfield. Adolescent images of Jamie and Lottie in the back of a car. Good grief Jamie! And highly fictionalized and enhanced recollections of an evening we spent in the Central Library after the doors were locked.'

'That actually happened!' I insisted. (Lottie was a librarian.)

'Your memory of what happened between the Romance and History stacks never happened! Nor between Fashion and Aerobics! I seem to remember we sat between with our backs to the Philosophy of Education and Mathematics shelves and mostly talked.'

'That was when I learnt I could count on you,' I said, instinctively.

'Very funny,' she said. 'I am leaving now.'

'Sorry,' I said.

'You need to move on.'

'Yes.'

'Stop re-living the past.'

'Fair point.'

'And stop fantasizing about me.'

'Right.'

'It is not good for you and it is disgusting.'

Lottie nodded at Keziah again and strode off.

I put my head inside the open door and quickly looked around behind the wall. 'I'll just close this,' I said to Keziah.

We walked on. Lottie's determined stride was fast taking her out of sight behind a hill.

Keziah and I then shared a rather full pause during which Keziah didn't say anything, because without saying anything Keziah had already said everything.

Here is what Keziah didn't need to say as we silently tramped:

'These are memories of your ex-girlfriend.'

'They may be.'

'Who is now married to someone else and living on another continent.'

'I suppose.'

'They are taking up more and more room on your soul.'

'Things grow. You adjust.'

'Is it healthy to devote so much of your soul to reliving your time with this woman who has left you for someone else?'

'That's an arguable point.'

'Or fantasising about a different history.'

'Well—'

Keziah would then have sniffed a sniff of contempt.

As it was, the conversation and sniff were unnecessary but I felt just as vaguely cross as if we had had the conversation and she had sniffed the sniff.

It was a relief to move to her soul, which we did easily because it was moored next to mine against the pavement café at the *Diner*.

Keziah's soul is like a wedge-shaped weather-blasted island in the North Atlantic. At the pointy end is a moorland cottage from which she steers. We walked past this, and her whole triangular landscape opened before us: a bleak mountain plateau, sloping downward. In the distance stood a range of volcanoes, some of them smoking. Beyond them, I knew, was a scree slope, lakes, and a greener lower part leading to the far edge.

The feature you can't miss, like the crease in a paper aeroplane, is the geological scar running almost from the cottage to the mountains.

The scar had been carved first by Keziah's mother's cruel indifference and then cut deeper by the years of abuse at Keziah's boarding school.

Rain or no, I didn't think it would ever heal.

We trod along the stony path from the cottage, reedy grass and stones all around. It was misty. Keziah was alert.

'Down!' she suddenly said, pushing me behind a large rock.

'Ow!' I shook her off.

Then I heard a machine gun. Sharp pieces pinged off the rock.

I joined Keziah crouching behind the rock.

'I told you to get down,' said Keziah.

'Someone's shooting at us!'

'Really.'

With a moment of thought, Keziah had imagined up her own semi-automatic weapon, and she took off the safety. 'Shush.'

Cautiously she crawled to the edge of the rock and looked around. She took aim and fired.

The machine gun answered back.

'She cannot resist a fight,' muttered Keziah. 'She can never resist.'

'Who is it?' I asked.

But Keziah and who-ever-it-was were busy exchanging more metal.

'I just have to show her I'm not budging,' said Keziah. Then turned and shot again. 'She'll go back into her cave.'

'Who will?' I asked.

They swapped a few more sisterly rounds.

'Good,' said Keziah. 'She's got the idea.'

I risked a look, keeping my head down, and spotting a slight, pale girl, with shoulder-length black hair, a huge gun slung over her shoulders. She climbed nimbly down the vertical face of the scar and then swung herself into a cave.

'She looks just like you!'

'That's because she is me.'

'You are your own worst enemy.'

Keziah did not dignify this insight with a response.

'You should tell her, the machine gun suits her,' I said. 'Makes her look like some kind of sexy radical insurgent.'

'Shut up and come on.'

'Is it safe?'

'No.'


We trod along the stony path, the scar to our left, with the other Keziah down there in a cave somewhere.

'How come she's you?' I asked.

'I actually do think my soul is changing a bit,' Keziah replied. "There are flowers on this landscape now.'

'I noticed,' I said. Meagre moorland stuff, even goats would choke on them, but yes, technically, flowers.

'And look at that tree. That wasn't there before.' She pointed to a shrub that had pushed itself up through the scar. 'It has fruit. Look.'

She climbed watchfully down into the scar and tugged at a handful of berries that were nestled in a spiny branch. She clambered back up to me. 'Here.'

I took one from her open palm and cautiously tasted it.

'Peppery. Tangy. I see what you mean.'

'I didn't used to produce that. And part of me'— she nodded down in the direction of the cave— 'doesn't approve.'

'She's a reaction to the way your soul is changing.'

'She thinks I'm getting soft.'

'You?'

'And she thinks I'll get hurt again.'

'Ah.'

*Enough already about feelings.*

We started to climb the volcanic slopes. Passing volcanoes on either side, we scrambled down scree, then reached a tarn scooped into the shoulder of the mountain. Our path followed the water's edge, then threaded down the mountain into a valley that was sharp with reedy grass. From there we crossed a stream on a plank and clambered over a stile into a meadow. The meadow formed the far edge of Keziah's soul and was dotted with plants growing in labelled ceramic pots.

I knew this place was where Keziah organised her relationships, one per pot. She kept them here to stop them being destroyed by the flying rocks and flowing lava from the volcanoes. Even so, many pots were broken.

My eyes searched out the pot marked *Jamie*, which I thought was still pitifully small, and the plant she cultivated there was stumpy and leafy and with no fruit.

Nearby was a pot labelled *Mark*. Neat and compact, it held a tree like a silver birch, already twenty feet tall, white and elegant. Still firmly bound in a pot.

Interesting.

I wondered for a moment why Mark was bothering with Keziah, even if he ever got anywhere. Legions of leggy, horsey girls, well educated, tributes to British dentistry, would be eager to share a table and a bed with him. Why was he spurning them and slogging through the depression and anger that hung round Keziah like needy relatives?

'It's the fruit,' I suddenly said to myself.

'What?' asked Keziah.

'Nothing,' I said. 'Have we done our job now? What can we say? No obvious examples of enemy infiltration.'

'If we could even tell what that looks like,' said Keziah.

'I suppose.'

'Jonah and Corrie should be here when we get back,' said Keziah. 'I think they wanted to talk,'

'I'm still not totally sure I'm on board with this,' I said.

# DEFENSIVE FEASTING

Corrie Bright and the Prophet Jonah were our rescuers, mentors, and line managers, but they were hands-off to a worrying degree. The four of us were the only humans involved in soul care for Cambridge city; Keziah and I were only months into the job; Keziah had psychopathic leanings, and was a risk to herself and others, and me; but Jonah and Corrie left us to ourselves, not troubling us much beyond our weekly meetings.

So this was an exception.

We stepped off Keziah's soul, back onto the *Diner*, and saw Corrie, Jonah and Stub seated at a table on the pavement café. Kirsty had surrounded this table with two long tables and two short tables arranged in a loose rectangle. The tables were crowded with food.

We wandered over. Corrie's spirit was thin and birdlike with wispy hair and the blotched complexion of great age. She wore her old-lady kit of skirt and blouse and cardigan. Jonah was dark, lean, weathered and in a cheap suit. If you ever saw him walk he had a nautical gait, bow-legged and rolling, which was odd because he disliked ships. His eyes were gloomy and his eyebrows fidgeted.

Stub, still in hat and coat, had just a glass of plain water in front of him.

The food looked astonishing.

'Where's Kirsty?' I said to no-one. 'I need to worship the ground she walks on. *Look* at this.'

'We started,' said Jonah. This was unnecessary, given the dismembered giant crab on his plate.

I did manage to nod to Stub, give Corrie a kiss and shake Jonah's hand. Then I seized a plate and consciously tried to breathe evenly. A person facing an all-you-can-eat buffet needs to remember to breathe.

'I see what she's done,' I marvelled. 'Indian down one table. Chinese down the other. But then the two short tables … that's breads and creamy curries with lots of nuts and raisins, North Indian food, then noodles and dumplings and lots of mutton, Nepali and Tibetan food, and then edging down to … here we are … Sichuan cuisine onto the long Chinese table which must mean, excuse me, I'll just edge past, that the *other* short table navigates the long way back through Thai Green Curry and Malaysian Laksa across the Andaman Sea to, here we are, the coconut and fish curries of Sri Lanka and South India.'

I set my shoulders and stepped towards the mutton-stuffed bread known as a murtabak (Afghan food, first short table, top left). Most worthwhile cuisine sparkles against a murtabak backdrop. If the curries of the world were an English cottage garden in the high summer, murtabak would be the green lawn.

When I sat down a few minutes later, I had spooned onto my murtabak a modest batch of initial curries and added an onion bhaji and a samosa on the side.

(It's a judgement call, I agree. Too many starters—not to mention indiscipline among the poppadoms—can slow you at the third or fourth plateful. But on balance I thought it would be OK.)

'Stub said something about imminent destruction,' I said, though I was already feeling better about everything.

'A rumour of a threat of imminent destruction,' clarified Stub.

Jonah was seated across the plank table from me and he disposed of a king prawn which had been eyeing him steadily. The prophet, hook-nosed, oily-skinned, world-weary, pulled some pink mollusc exoskeleton from his teeth.

'Stub's right,' he said. 'Vanity Fair might be preparing to attack you. But they don't want to.'

'They don't?'

'They're middle-management. They just want to go about their business. That's how you survive in a bureaucracy.'

'I know those managers.'

'Yes you do: the Bull, the Sphinx, the Black Dog, and the Scary Haired Woman with all the arms. They've got their business managing Vanity Fair with its little rides and all the souls queuing up. And they offer advice and take their cut of the profits and everyone's happy.'

'Everyone except the human souls,' put in Corrie Bright.

'Who are being hollowed out like chairs infested with woodworm. Yes,' said Jonah. 'But anyway. Along comes Mark. Word comes down to the managers, from somewhere in the senior realms. Corrie's great-nephew is a troublemaker. He cruises from one influential meeting to another, meets one strategic contact after another. They are instructed to stop him.'

'Excuse me while I just explore the foods of North West China for a moment,' I interrupted, noticing my plate was thinning. Jonah resumed when I returned. I had ladled on some siu zhu pork, sesame cold noodle and spicy fried rice. I'd also edged over to the Indian table and scooped up some vada curry and chicken kotthu barotta from the Tamil end.

'They were happy when Mark was building technology companies,' said Jonah. 'Not now he's got an interest in the poor. Don't miss the lamb biryani—Indian table near the top.'

'I'd planned that for plate number four,' I said. 'Perhaps I should bump it up to three.'

'I would,' said Jonah. 'Defensive feasting.'

'I could swap the biryani for the Tibetan dumpling which I was beginning to feel unsure about anyway.'

'Wise. The managers of Vanity Fair are not blessed with original minds,' continued Jonah. 'And normally they don't *need* original minds. They just organize the fairground and wait for human souls to bankrupt themselves.'

'But in this case?'

'In our case the four managers are probably being leaned on to take some initiative. Not just wait around.'

'They'll probably go for all of you,' put in Corrie Bright. 'You're a unit.'

'Oh.' Unpleasant as it was, that made sense. Mark's money was backing Michael's Oyster Café. I was working for both of them. Keziah was going to move her law office to the Oyster Café. Mark was dating Keziah. And Keziah and I had a part-time role defending souls in the heavenlies.

'They can unravel the whole network by attacking any part of it,' said Jonah.

'Just as Mark's trying to unravel *their* whole network by attacking parts of it,' I added. 'Even though he doesn't know that's what he's doing.'

'As I said, they won't like this,' said Jonah. 'So what do they do? I think they'll probably just stick to what they know.'

'Which is?'

'The full-on assault,' said Corrie.

'Oh. How do they … What do they do?'

'Exploit your weaknesses,' said Corrie. 'Pick at the scabs on your soul.'

'If I have any.'

'Indeed,' said Corrie, 'or if they aren't too spoilt for choice.'

'But none of this might be happening anyway?' I said hopefully. 'You only suspect.'

'There was much chatter about it in the regions around Vanity Fair, sir,' put in Stub. 'And considerable pleasure. The lesser beings always enjoy seeing those more powerful under pressure.'

'So you think something's brewing.'

'I do.'

'So … so what do we do?'

Jonah removed more prawn bits. 'Not much we can do,' he said. 'Except wait.'

'Wait for a full-on assault of powerful spiritual beings on our souls?' I asked.

'There's a couple of things,' added Corrie. 'You can keep more of an eye on your own souls, and Mark's and Michael's. And we can ask Stub to find out what he can.'

'As you may know, sir,' added Stub, 'some species of heavenly being fly from soul to soul like scavenger birds or butterflies. They trade in information. They are rather amoral in whom they trade with.'

'And,' continued Corrie, 'Kirsty can monitor the gossip network, see if anything is happening on earth that might be relevant. Stub? You should report anything to me and we can see if Jonah and I need to come and help. Meanwhile I wonder if you two' – she nodded at Keziah and I—'shouldn't visit Mark and Michael?'

'Should we be worried?' I asked.

'Being worried would be good,' said Jonah. 'But it'll probably work out.'

Bolstered by the foods of the East, I could have half believed he was right.

The magnificent meal ended. Corrie updated us with the names of a few other souls we should give attention to over the next couple of nights, and then she and Jonah left us.

Jonah spent a lot of his time in a still higher heavenly dimension, the University of Metanarratives, where he and other senior types were trying to housetrain the cultural discourses of the whole nation. Corrie, meanwhile, mostly watched the heavens, endlessly swapping filters and perspectives, following the changing spiritual seasons.

Today, however, Corrie and Jonah told us they were heading back to a repeat job on the soul of a researcher who was still puzzling over the cancer-bashing properties of a monoclonal antibody.[1]

They told us to keep in touch.

---

[1] Scientists at Cambridge's MRC laboratory have won four Nobel Prizes since 2000.

I enjoy sitting among the ruins of a meal, but Keziah got up.

'That was quite something,' I mused.

Keziah said nothing, collecting her bag from under the chair. 'I mean Kirsty is awesome but I thought she climbed new heights tonight.'

'It's pathetic how easy you are to steer,' said Keziah.

'What do you mean?'

'You're totally stomach-driven. Why do you think Kirsty made that meal?'

I considered this. 'I imagine it's something to do with her having a generous and hospitable nature. This may not be a familiar concept.'

'It was to stop you being peevish.'

'I'm never peevish.'

'If they'd have said, "Vanity Fair are arming for war and you need to man up and face them," you know what you'd've been like.'

'I'd've manned up.'

'You'd have whined. We'd have wasted half an hour at least. Whereas all they need to do is feed you and you'll do whatever they want.'

'I thought on the whole that was a good thing.'

'You've got the moral fibre of a cornflake.'

'However, unlike some people, I have a kindly and warm personality.'

'Come on,' said Keziah. 'We've got to get to work.'

'Who are we going to do first?'

'Mark and Michael.'

# THE SOUL OF A VENTURE CAPITALIST

How do you find stuff in the heavens? Keziah and I were getting good at this now. You borrow a chariot and pengub from the *Diner* garage. You drive—or Keziah usually drives because she is a disruptive passenger in chariots as she is in life—to a big lighthouse in the heavens. Called the Enlightenhouse, a copy of it is always visible wherever you are in the heavenly places. You moor your chariot and climb the Enlightenhouse's stairs. Each time you come to a window, you tell the window to block out some of the information in the heavens. Then you climb some more.

Finally, you have blocked out all the information you don't need. The soul you want will then be somewhere in sight. You lean out of the window, wave to the pengub, climb into your chariot again, and fly to the soul.

So to find Mark we tried to say *Venture Capitalists* at one window (we were already in the Cambridge Space). That would have isolated all but a few dozen souls. But they were hard to pick out because they were scattered over such a wide area of the heavens.

I was going to try *Happy Venture Capitalists* at the next window, but Keziah gave me a dismissive push and said *Venture Capitalists called Mark* which did eliminate all but a couple and from there it was easy to pick out Mark Bright.

We climbed into our chariot and set off to catch up with him.

Mark's soul was like a yacht, white, neat, gleaming. He had hoisted a mainsail, jib and spinnaker since I had last seen him. With the pengub pulling him at one angle, and the sails pushing slightly at another--remember your vectors—the ship of his soul flew forward, squeezed between the desire of his heart which pulled and some random breeze in the heavens that pushed. A steered, driven man. The pengub and his soul each splashed through blobs of golden rain like pacmen eating rows of dots. Our poor *Diner* pengub had to sprint to get close to him.

We peeked inside portholes as we drew alongside and saw that several decks were stocked with memories, good education, wide reading and comfortable upbringing.

We moored against an open deck and climbed aboard.

Mark would not have been a good subject for fiction because this deck, like the rest of his soul, was trimmed of clutter, open, and seemingly lacking in dark spaces, gaping cracks, or wandering monsters.

Finding some stairs, we climbed towards his bridge. We passed a stateroom and looked through one of its glass doors: a number of ideas—some I recognized—sat at a conference table, ready to give presentations whenever Mark was ready to meet them.

We climbed to the bridge itself, opened the door a smidgeon and looked through. Mark had tied the ship's wheel to maintain his course and was examining a chart.

We watched for a while, then closed the door again and trod back down the stairs.

'I don't see *any* vulnerabilities,' I said, once we were out of earshot. 'I used to. You remember. Before he gave up his old job that stateroom was chaotic, ideas all over the place. And that teenage idea called Frenzie playing the drums on his bridge, disrupting his whole life. Now that he's taken the plunge, she's all sorted. He's like one of the cool kids at school who was always good at everything.'

While I was talking away, I noticed we passed a door in the corridor labelled

PROJECT 'K'.

The door was closed. We passed it quickly, and maybe Keziah didn't notice it. This is possible because she is not the kind of person who looks brightly around places as she trudges through life. Or perhaps she *did* notice something but didn't choose to say. In any case she was busy disagreeing with me as we started to climb down the final set of steps to the open deck again:

'I don't know how anybody can be so wrong!'

'He definitely *is* one of the cool kids and his soul is in a good place. He's miles from Vanity Fair. I've hardly ever been this high in the heavens.'

'Faults! Everything's wooden.' She ticked things off on her stubby fingers. 'Proud. Self-sufficient. Smug. And probably emotionally not at home.'

'And sort of your boyfriend,' I put in, foolishly ignoring Kirsty's advice not to mention this.

'Irrelevelant,' snapped Keziah. (That's not a misprint. She struggles over long words with lots of 'l's and 'r's. It's almost endearing.) 'We're at work.'

'In any case,' I said, as I followed her back into the chariot, 'I don't see a gaping vulnerability to Vanity Fair.'

'Any of us can crash and burn.'

'Michael next? He's definitely not one of the cool kids.'

We climbed on board the chariot and she snapped the reins.

'Weeee! down!' said the pengub's speech bubble.

# THE REFORMER

Rumpled, battered, gangly, Michael, the widower, so it was said, of an unpleasant wife, was not a person ever accused of being distant or perfectionist.

Somehow he was a cleric also, and perhaps that was saving his soul. There wasn't a sin he hadn't been tempted to, or a discipline he had entirely kept with. He was always late, sociable, kind, clever, sympathetic, forgiving, broken, repentant, weary and tinged with sadness.

Keziah once told me that when the Probation Service prepare reports on criminals in the Magistrates' Courts, they assess the risk of future offending. You would assess Michael as being at high risk of future offending.

And yet he hadn't.

Keziah and I knew his soul well because we had worked intensively there several months ago. Most of it is a cathedral, though there are also outlying villages. We landed our chariot as usual on the cathedral lawn. Offices and Michael's home also surrounded this carpet of grass. We glanced quickly around.

Michael used the offices for his various projects. I suspected when one office grew too cluttered, he opened a new one, working his way down the row. He kept personal memories in his many-bedroomed home. He worshipped in the cathedral. Around the back of the house, we knew, were some allotments, his place of whimsy. Burrowed into the slopes between the allotment and the cathedral were a series of tunnels, where over the lonely years he had dug out long corridors of a fantasy life.

'I think he's probably in one of the offices,' I said to Keziah. 'I can see a light on.'

'Otherwise quiet,' she replied. 'And quite tidy for him.'

Without needing to consult we climbed from the chariot and walked between the house and the offices, down the cart-track to his allotments.

Ideas—they looked like vegetables—grew in his allotment, but few of them bore fruit. Some needed pruning; some were entangled with other ideas; some should have been supported with sticks and string; most, you had no idea what they were, amusing and quirky plants.

'The tunnels are still blocked up,' I said. Keziah and I had filled them in months ago, stopping the fantasies from overflowing into his outer life. Shortly after that we'd introduced Michael to Mark, and his soul and his Oyster Café project had done well ever since.

'No footprints either,' I said. 'I don't think he's been coming back.'

'Music's still going on though,' said Keziah. In the tunnels, the bass notes of a party still throbbed.

'If you were Vanity Fair, wouldn't you attack here?' I asked Keziah.

She shrugged. 'Or you or me or all of us at once.'

But all was quiet.

We headed back for the chariot to the handful of soul visits that were the rest of our night's work

*

Nothing happened for a week.

It was, I reflected one night in bed, nine months since our crash. My journey since then had been more zig-zaggy than Keziah's and had three parts. *Medical appointments and health scares.* These were slowly tailing off. *Physical restoration.* I was no longer struggling through the streets being tailgated by people with walking frames. *Self-confidence.* I had grown slowly less scared about leaving the house; working at Madge's had been a big breakthrough.

The emotions were still wrecked though. Which was possibly why I still sought solace with Lottie, slipping over the wall in my soul to be with my memories and dreams of her.

I knew I had to behave myself. Keziah would be inspecting. However my favourite thing was quite innocent: just to walk with my memories of Lottie.

I liked a beach best. The two of us would be bare-legged, holding hands, squashing wet footmarks in the sand. We would walk in that awkward way that came from her being taller than I and with a different stride. Everything was softened by the lapping sea and the warm breeze. Occasionally, wormcasts would trouble us. And we would argue.

Lottie, like someone else once said of his friend, had read most of the right books but had got the wrong thing out of each one. She was the same with people— she'd completely misunderstood everyone. Where I'd seen aggression or bumptiousness, she'd seen insecurity. Where I'd seen a militant vegan and armed myself appropriately, she'd seen a sister, lonely and unloved.

Yet when I pointed out her errors, rather than listening like a proper girlfriend, she would dismiss *my* insights and pile straight back with hers. As if I hadn't understood anything.

We could make a disagreement last half a wide bay.

Sometimes as we argued I glanced across at her, all animated, and wondered what love with someone like her would be like—being deeply known by her *and* being welcomed in her life, both at the same time.

Would have been nice to find out.

# A PLANNING DILEMMA

'Nothing,' I said.

Jonah, Corrie, Stub, Keziah and I were meeting at a table at the *Shepherd Diner* and Corrie had asked us if anything had happened in the week since we last met. It was warm at the *Diner*, and Kirsty had delivered smoothies and fresh fruit and salty snacks.

Before arriving, Keziah and I had already re-visited our own souls again, and Mark's and Michael's.

'I remain sure they are planning something,' said Stub. 'There is definitely traffic between your souls and Vanity Fair.'

'I'm sure that's not happening to me,' I said. 'I'd notice.'

'I'm bound to say I'm sure it is, sir,' said Stub. 'Have you not lain asleep and felt a coldness steal over your soul or a dark shadow fall? Hasn't a thought ever dropped into your dreams that you knew was totally alien? Have you not felt something tugging at a memory like a bird digging out a worm?'

'So why haven't Vanity Fair unleashed their forces of horror?' asked Jonah, eyeing suspiciously his reddish fruit-filled smoothie and its frothy head. 'Let's speculate.'

'Number 1,' said Keziah (her smoothie: tall, mint green, chocolate flake bars and ice cubes). 'Perhaps they're still gathering information and perfecting their plans.'

'Good,' said Jonah approvingly.

'Number 2. Maybe they're arguing among themselves.'

'Also possible,' said Jonah. 'Anything else?'

'Number 3. Something we haven't thought of.'

'How can we think of something we haven't thought of?' I asked (mango, chocolate, fresh raspberries and chilli). Keziah didn't even spare me a withering look.

'They want to stop the Oyster Café project. And drown us in the Sump of Lost Dreams? So why not attack someone else?' suggested Keziah.

'Such as who?' I asked.

'Why is the planning officer in the council being so awkward?' asked Keziah.

'Huh,' I said. 'Perhaps he's just an awkward character.'

'Why couldn't Vanity Fair be getting at him instead? If you want to stop the project, stop the plans.'

'It is good to have a lawyer among us,' I said, half-admiring. 'Should we ever feel the lack of Low Cunning.'

'I'm criminal, not commercial,' said Keziah. 'My clients don't usually do Low Cunning, more Unbelievable Stupidity.'

'Even so,' I said. 'There's a gift there.'

'It's possible,' said Jonah, still eyeing his smoothie with a suspicious eye. 'But I don't think so this time. Corrie?'

'It's a stretch,' said Corrie (black beer).

'This is the Bull, the Sphinx, the Black Dog and the Scary Haired Woman. "Strategic" is a bit of a leap for them,' said Jonah.

'So the planning officer could just be being unreasonable without prompting from them,' said Keziah. 'Fair enough. I had an idea though.'

'Is this number 4 in your list?' I asked.

'No,' said Keziah. 'This is a job for you.'

'Oh, thank you very much.'

'It does involve a meal, though. Michael. We know he's a vulnerable kind of character. And he's especially vulnerable if his hopes are broken down. We also know he's a lot less vulnerable when he's full of vision for something and thinks it's actually going to happen.'

'So?'

'So take him out for lunch. Get him to talk about the Oyster Café. Don't let him get bogged down thinking it's all going to end badly.'

'Doesn't sound too bad.'

'Strengthen his spiritual immune system.'

'It's a bit unfocussed,' I said. 'But I suppose since it involves a meal, it's worth a try.'

'One other thing,' said Corrie, after pecking delicately at her milk stout. 'I think Jamie and I should do the visits to Mark's soul for a while.'

Keziah reddened. 'Not necessary. I'm fine. I'm focussed. I'm professional.'

'Indulge an old lady,' said Corrie.

'Honestly I'm fine.'

'Still,' said Corrie.

Keziah looked mutinous, but with a great effort managed to swallow any further argument.

'Clearly needs the top team to take it from here,' I told her.

*

Another day, and a night, and still our souls remained unattacked by heavenly hordes.

We continued our heavenly business.

On earth, the planning for the Oyster Café slowly went forward.

What were they doing?

# A SUSHI SHOP

The next day, on earth, I took Michael to a sushi shop just off Market Square. Sushi shops are in many ways the next step in the road to the perfect meal, the all-you-can-eat plus a conveyor belt.

Chopsticks wielded, empty bowls building up around us, it was time to get on with it. Operation Build Up Michael's Spiritual Immune system. Ready for the attack that—I knew and he didn't know—was coming.

'It's nice to get some time to talk,' I said. 'Outside of work. So what gets you out of bed in a morning? To go out Vicaring for another day?'

'My prostate usually,' said Michael. 'If you can avoid ever being in your sixties, do.'

'I'll make a note. I don't even know what Vicars do, flower rotas? Dying people? That kind of thing?'

'It can happen,' said Michael. 'We're working to a job description that's about 500 years old—one all-rounder in every parish. It works OK if you like studying or teaching; or caring for people. If you're a skilled manager? Not so easy to use your skills. Or an entrepreneur? Even harder.

'I've been lucky, but it took a long time. They finally gave me Madge's which is small, but in the city centre and that gave me scope to be what I really wanted.'

'Which is?'

'Half a vicar, and half a founder of start-ups. But even here that didn't work initially.'

'Why not?'

'Churches are insidious. A million small jobs. And an ethic of love. Very hard to say no to people. So I didn't get as much time for the entrepreneurship as I would have liked.'

We paused to watch a tray of dumplings pass.

Michael didn't know this, but Keziah and I had visited his soul a few months ago, just about at its lowest point. We'd seen the shabby cathedral. We'd seen a graveyard of aborted hopes and plans. We'd seen the secret fantasy life to which he'd turned.

'So that's why it was so timely meeting Mark. He'd been on a completely separate journey and we found we each had two halves of a vision. It was like a band getting together.'

*You have no idea*, I thought.

'In retrospect, it's what happens all over Cambridge. Ideas and business skills meet. And Mark was coming from the commercial space into the social enterprise space. And I was waiting for him.'

I felt a little surge of pride that up in the heavens we hadn't been totally barren.

'So what happens it if doesn't work?' I asked. 'If the plans are turned down? Have you got a plan for that? A no-plan plan?'

'Not really,' said Michael.

'So what's your biggest fear?'

Michael paused and his eyes momentarily betrayed him. I knew his biggest fear. Moral collapse and disgrace.

'My biggest fear?' He cast around a bit, I thought. 'We Christians have a terrible habit of calling a small success a triumph. And then letting our original big vision fly away like a balloon. One of my bigger fears would be failing mildly enough so as to re-badge it as a success.'

I nodded. 'Wouldn't satisfy.'

'No,' said Michael. 'And sometimes—in my best moments—it feels like my life has been heading toward this. This has a better feel to it than anything I've done for a long time. It's a good feeling.

*And please keep holding that thought, Michael.*

'I bet it is,' I agreed.

'And what about you?' Michael continued.

'What about me?'

'Your dreams. *I* dream of something that genuinely fills the gaps in our provision for the needy and the homeless and the addicted. Something that takes state provision, which is very patchy, and charitable provision, which is also patchy, and sews them into an actual safety net. What about you? What do you dream about?'

My turn to lie.

'I depends what I've been watching before I go to bed.'

Michael was not to be put off.

'One thing, Tiger. One wish. What would you like?'

(Michael had the annoying habit of nicknaming people. He called Keziah 'Sixpence'. Hugely to her embarrassment.)

I was fairly honest, but I didn't mention Lottie.

'Honestly? I'd quite like not to be broken any more,' I said. 'You get weary of it. Every day. You want a holiday from the long-term project of putting yourself back together.'

I didn't know if this would spark Michael into full counselling mode. It could happen, given his vicarness (or is it vicarity?). So I added quickly, 'Working at Madge's has been good though. Another piece in the jigsaw. But I'd still prefer not to have been broken up in the first place.'

'Do you blame Keziah for all this?'

'Totally. It was her fault.'

'But you talk to her sometimes.'

'We've kept in touch.'

'She's a treasure. I know a number of lawyers, but no-one like her.'

'She's certainly a fighter,' I said. 'Not so good when a fight is not needed, however.'

'I wonder if she and Mark will make a go of it?'

'I hope so,' I said. 'Not totally sure what Mark gets from the deal.'

'I do,' said Michael.

'What?' I asked.

'Blood and fire,' said Michael with a smile. 'If he has milk in his veins she will replace it with rocket fuel.'

'Good luck with that,' I said.

# EURRGH

The attack came that night, and I almost didn't realize.

It was a mega-sleepless night, and before I knew it my head was full of Lotties. They were swarming all over it, all the memories and dreams I'd ever had about her, the sweet ones and the … creative ones.

As if a wall on my soul had broken down.

I got up, had a cup of tea, went back to bed. Still couldn't tame my head. Through my mind, the Lotties swarmed. And, let's be honest, writhed and giggled.

As 3:00 inched around to 4:00, and I was drowning in all my fantasy Lotties, a flare of common sense fired.
*Phone Keziah.*
*You are joking,* I thought to myself.
*Phone Keziah.*
*Shan't. Out of the question. I cannot face this. I won't.*
So I lay in bed in the darkness looking at my phone. I had a knot in my stomach.
*Shan't.*
*Shan't.*
*Shan't.*

3:31 am. I closed my eyes, pressed the phone key.

'I'm really sorry to bother you,' I said.

'Jamie. Thank you,' said Keziah.

'What?'

'I've been sitting here for the past half hour with a phone in my hand.'

'You have?'

'Something wrong with my head. Overwhelming. Gloom and anger.'

'*You* were going to ring *me*?'

'Yes.'

'And I rang you first?'

'Yes.'

'Figures. Somebody had to step up.'

Keziah took a moment to melt my phone with a curse.

'Fair point,' I said. 'Do you think this is it? The attack?'

'There's an idea Jamie,' said Keziah.

'What are we going to do?'

'Fight.'

'Is that your response to everything?'

'Yes.' Then she added, in a tone of voice that implied, *I would rather say anything than this thing I am about to say.* 'Fight them together. We clearly can't fight on our own.'

I groaned as one in pain.

'I'll come to you,' said Keziah. 'Then you can come to me. Where are you?'

'My soul may possibly be pulled around towards some of the rides in Vanity Fair. You?'

'Same. Different rides. I think I probably know the general area you're heading,' said Keziah. 'I'll find you.'

*Oh goody.* I clicked my phone off, disembodied my spirit with a little shrug and flickered onto my soul. When I got my bearings and looked out of the window, I saw that my soul was in the queue for one of the rollercoasters in Vanity Fair: The Fantasy Obsession. I had fallen a long way.

With great reluctance I took a folding chair from the groundskeepers' room and sat on it on my cricket field, waiting for Keziah.

Fantasy Jamies-and-Lotties were scattered all over the edge of the field. I'll draw a veil over what they were doing. They looked up at me briefly, then resumed their work.

This was deeply awful.

But at least I'd phoned Keziah, which, miserable option though it was, was the right thing.

So long as she hurried.

The heavens above my cricket field were garish, and birds were tweeting. Above me, a feathery wisp of cloud tangled itself with a second one. A third joined it. Slowly these tufts assembled themselves into a big shaggy raincloud.

Then another accumulated next to it. And a third. Soon there was a fat herd of them, black and white, filling the darkening sky.

I heard a muffled throaty roar. Keziah's chosen vehicle for hopping between soul-landscapes was her motorbike, and it dropped out of the sky and bounced onto the field.

She had presumably returned to her soul, picked up the motorbike, and buzzed off across the heavens in search of me.

The instant tyre met turf, sheet lightening lit up the sky from one end to the other. Keziah brought the bike to a halt, climbed off, and was tugging at her helmet when a long peal of thunder rolled across the landscape.

All over the field the Jamies and Lotties were standing up, pulling some clothes on, straightening others, fixing their hair, wrapping up picnics, taking each other by the hand, and running for the hills.

Too late. A downpour of gold-lit rain tumbled from the sky onto us all like a trove of pennies.

Keziah ambled over to me, not without a little swagger. Like me, like everyone, she was instantly drenched. We could hardly see the Jamies and Lotties through the curtain of glinting water. They were running for cover.

We watched them together, enjoying the rain.

'How did you do that?' I asked. 'It was like the Second Coming.'

'I have to admit it was probably you,' said Keziah. 'When you found the guts to ring me, you unleashed all this.'

'Where are they all going?' she asked.

'Back to Lottie-land, I suppose.'

'That's no good.'

'Why not?' I asked.

'They're just going to break out again. Come on.' She marched towards the hills.

'Look, they're fine there,' I insisted, following. 'Leave them be. Problem sorted.'

'Not sorted,' she said, and trod off, heading over moor and fen, o'er crag and torrent.

'Your problem is, you never know when to stop,' I muttered as we strode up a hill.

We reached the walls of Lottie-land on my soul. As far as I could tell, every fantasy Jamie-and-Lottie had fled there and presumably disappeared behind the wall. Still the torrents fell.

A hole had been blasted in the wall. Hovering above the rubble was a woman with straggly black hair, black teeth, many arms, and a sullen look. Black mascara was running. Drenched, she was scowling at the rain. Her gossamer wings were whirring.

'I'm going! I'm going!' she said, flapping her wings so hard they became a blur and gave off a low rasping noise. She rose into the air, fell back, rose again, fell again, and finally buzzed into the sky and through the clouds.

We watched her. At the same time, I could feel my whole soul rising as it lifted itself out of Vanity Fair towards the higher heavens.

I was silent for some time, trying to untangle the mix of shame, relief and embarrassment I was feeling, and trying to hide it all from Keziah.

'Thank you,' I said finally.

'You're welcome,' said Keziah.

'I'm glad that's over.'

'It isn't over. You need to get rid of this whole feature,' nodding with her head at Lottie-land behind the wall.

'I was *attacked*,' I said. 'That Scary Haired Woman demolished the wall. It's just like Jonah said. I was fine till then.'

'You were not fine. You were an accident waiting to happen. You need to totally re-landscape this.'

'Arguably.'

'Software,' said Keziah, unexpectedly. 'If a developer found a vulnerability that was being exploited, what would they do?'

'Patch it,' I said.

'So that the vulnerability can't be exploited. Yes.'

Keziah was learning to talk to me in terms I understood, namely computer programs. Oh no you don't.

'I will patch it by rebuilding the wall,' I said. 'And then we can get onto your soul. And sort that out.'

'It's not enough.'

'It will do.'

She glowered at me while I rebuilt the wall, not helping.

The rain slowed, then stopped, leaving my soul glistening.

'Come on,' she said eventually. 'We'll have to get this over with.'

We hiked back to the cricket field and climbed onto her motorbike.

# ALT-KEZIAH

There is a pleasant way for two people of opposite sexes to ride a motorbike. The pleasant way involves a man up front, a young woman behind, and she wrapping her arms around his waist and laying her head against his back. He revs the engine, and everyone is wearing leather.

The unpleasant way involves Keziah steering, neither of us wanting to touch the other, and me being terrified.

We had flown to a gloomier region of Vanity Fair. Rides loomed out of the darkness as we buzzed along.

'The Dripping Tunnel,' said Keziah, steering us past a glistening entrance. 'That slurping noise is Self-Loathing dropping from the ceiling.'

A giant sponge appeared in the gloom, covered with stalks. Each stalk glistened with a gluey blob on its end. 'The Null Emotion Honeydew,' she explained, pulling at the handlebars to steer the flying bike upwards.

'You know this part of Vanity Fair?'

'Yes.'

'Seems very deep and a long way away.'

'Well-trodden mental path. There's my soul. Orbiting the Nameless Dark Place.'

'Sweet.'

Keziah steered the bike round to the back of her soul, where she aimed for a wide ledge in the cliff-face. The bike skidded to a stop and we clambered off.

Above us were about ten feet of loose rocks. Below, the steep cliff faced out into the heavens, which were crowded with the sullen rides of this part of Vanity Fair.

'This is the only bit of my soul I can call my own at the moment,' she said in response to my puzzled look. 'She's taken over.'

'Your whole soul? In one night? What are we going to do?'

Keziah started climbing the rock face, rather gingerly because some of the rocks were loose. She managed to get her head high enough to see the view and signalled for me to climb up alongside her.

We peered across a rock field to the meadow where she kept all the ceramic pots containing her relationships. All the pots had been piled together into one place, and a Black Dog was guarding them. He was sleeping.

We heard a clattering and clanking behind us and looked down. A pengubim-drawn chariot had landed on the ledge next to the motorbike. The prophet Jonah stepped out and then he helped Corrie Bright down. Keziah and I stumbled down the rock face and joined them.

'Hello my dear,' said the wizened Corrie, and gave Keziah a hug. 'Excuse us if we join you.'

'I don't know what happened,' said Keziah. 'Everything just overwhelmed me. Hasn't done that for months.'

'And your soul's just gone into a spiral,' said Jonah. 'If I was guessing I would say it will pick up speed around the Nameless Dark Place and head straight for a ride called the Mouth of Doom.'

'Is that bad?' I asked.

'The name might be a clue,' he said. 'It digests what it can of a soul and excretes what's left directly into the Sump of Lost Dreams. It's a whatsit, a check valve. Souls only go through it one way. That's unusual. Most of the Vanity Fair rides recycle souls so that they keep coming back.'

'So—' I said.

'Let's go over what happened,' said Corrie. 'Keziah. You were lying in bed and—'

'Mockery,' said Keziah. 'Like, what is the point of anything.'

'Anger?' asked Corrie.

'Oh yes.'

'And now a sense of pointlessness and futility? We saw the Black Dog just up there. All three at once.'

'*I* was attacked by that Scary Haired Woman with all the arms,' I said. 'Wasn't that difficult to get rid of her. Confession. Good for the soul.'

'Good,' said Corrie.

'So perhaps this is just as easy to fix.'

Corrie, Jonah and Keziah shared a look.

'I think possibly,' said Jonah, 'as a character you're not so *entrenched* as Keziah. In her personality.'

'You mean I'm healthier,' I said.

'Shallower may be another way of putting it,' said Jonah.

'Ah.'

'Jamie,' said Jonah. 'Could you make your way over to the big geological scar? See if anything's happening to it. Ideally, don't be seen.'

'What if I am seen?'

'If you're shot at, stamped on or bitten, try to recall that anything you feel at the time is probably not true. Ideally, though, don't be.'

'Oh. Right. You'd like me to go now?'

'And report back. Yes.'

'Now?'

'Please.'

'And what are you going to do?'

'I think we'll probably make Keziah a cup of tea.'

'Oh. Right then.'

'It's hard to think of anyone who will do this job quite like you Jamie,' said Corrie Bright.

They were all looking at me.

I set off.


It was easy enough sneaking past the sleeping Black Dog. I crossed the plank bridge from the meadow and started climbing up the scree.

Keziah's soul-landscape was grumbling and smoking. Every so often one of the volcanoes at the top of the ridge would blow, firing out smoke and rocks. I would shelter behind a rock until the rocks stopped falling and the smoke cleared.

I passed the tarn and kept climbing. As I did, I briefly glimpsed two figures on the skyline. They were walking down the path towards me—or one was; the other was hovering next to the first. I quickly left the path, scrambled over the scree and hid behind a formation of rocks.

I watched them pass. The striding figure was the alter-ego Keziah, tight-faced and slender, AK-47 on her hips. The other was a Sphinx, car-sized and the colour of ebony, using big swoops of his reptilian black wings to stay at her shoulder.

'We're not pleased,' said the Sphinx. 'She's been stable for months. And these flowers.'

'It hasn't been easy,' said the alt-Keziah.

'I shouldn't need to be doing this,' said the Sphinx. 'I've got a job to do in Vanity Fair.'

They jogged by. I waited a few more moments before resuming my hike. I kept my head down in case they looked back and spotted me against the skyline.

I crossed the mountain pass between two smoking volcanoes. The path snaked through the moorland to the edge of the geological scar, then ran alongside it. Sprays of stone and dirt were being thrown up from scar's depths.

I stepped cautiously along the edge of the scar until I found somewhere I could crouch down and peer over. Perhaps a hundred feet below, a Bull was charging. It rammed the side of the scar, gouged out stones and rocks, tossed them high. Squirmy orange worms wriggled in the loosened earth.

After each charge, the landscape shook and rumbled as if in pain.

I knew from earlier adventures this ground was loaded with Keziah's memories. Some she kept in cages down subterranean corridors. Others were buried. The Bull's rampage was leaving coffins half-exposed.

A flock of birds followed the Bull as it gored the scar. They were burrowing with their beaks and tossing more soil around.

I glanced up at the cottage from which Keziah steered her soul; far away, it looked forlorn and dark.

I'd seen enough and made my way back, detouring round one of the volcanoes, past a derelict village on the mountainside.

I eventually scrambled back down the rock face. Keziah, Jonah and Corrie Bright were sitting in folding chairs taken from the chariot. A picnic hamper was open between them. They looked up at me.

I was hot from my exertions and my clothes felt stiff with smoke.

'Ah Jamie,' said Corrie. 'We saved you some tea but I didn't think you were a big fan of sandwiches.'

'You've been having a picnic!' I said.

'Keziah was just getting her head in the right place. We're nearly done. Did you see anything?'

'It's like a First World War battlefield out there,' I said. 'There's a Bull all over your geological scar and I saw that alt-Keziah being advised by a Sphinx. The whole landscape keeps shaking and your volcanoes keep erupting.'

'All three of them, then,' said Corrie Bright. 'Anger, Mockery and Depression. Are you ready, Keziah?'

'I am,' said Keziah.

'Good,' continued Corrie. 'We'll put the picnic away and head off and then Jamie can follow you.'

'What's she going to do?' I asked.

'Reclaim her soul,' said Corrie. 'From its temporary eclipse. Your tea's a bit cold but you probably fancy a mouthful.'

'What was I doing all that for then? I was—it was dangerous.'

'Vital reconnoitring,' said Corrie.

'Vital. Appreciated,' added Jonah.

'And you kindly gave Keziah some headspace,' continued Corrie. 'Your tea. You can follow on a bit behind her after you've had a quick drink.'

'Aren't *you* going? Don't we need … an army or something?'

'We think she'll manage without an army,' said Jonah. 'She just really needed a cup of tea.'

With a familiar feeling of not being quite on top of things, I swallowed some tea, and then helped Jonah and Corrie pack up the chariot.

They flew off, a whirl of wheels. Keziah climbed the rocks again and motioned for me to join her. By the time I scrambled up, Keziah was striding across the meadow.

The Black Dog was sleeping. I saw her stop, raise her foot, and kick it.

The Dog yelped, jumped, ran away, turned around, ran towards Keziah, turned around again, ran away again, then decided to run around the pile of pots. He was barking in English: 'Rough! Rough! Def'nitley not right! Not right def'nitley! Rough! Rough! Not right!'

Keziah picked up a pot and moved it into the middle of the field, then fetched another, and a third. She seemed to be spreading them around so that she could tend each one individually rather than have them as an untidy pile.

She picked up Mark's pot, which had fallen over, and carefully straightened it.

Keeping an eye on the Dog, which was still running in circles and barking, I joined her.

'Where do these go?' I asked.

'Just give each a bit of room. Ah, here she comes.'

Keziah nodded to where alt-Keziah and the Sphinx were crossing the plank bridge. Alt-Keziah strode towards us, gun swinging from her hips, while the Sphinx flapped heavily at her shoulder.

'Just remember everything I told you,' said the Sphinx smoothly. 'I'm off back to the Fair. Management matters.'

The Dog stopped its barking for a moment and angled its head quizzically as the Sphinx stretched his wings and flew.

He started running about again. 'We're off? We're off? We're off?' Everyone ignored him. 'We're off!' he decided and jumped over the cliff.

'If she shoots you,' said Keziah quietly to me, 'just keep a clear head.'

'What?'

'Probably be just a flesh wound. I don't think much goes deep for you.'

'Oh.'

The alt-Keziah stopped a few paces away from Keziah. 'It can't happen for you Keziah. Trust me. I'm your friend.'

Keziah looked right back at her, eye to eye. 'You're not my friend.'

I was about to point out, 'Obviously true, because Keziah doesn't have *any* friends,' but decided to stay tactfully silent.

The alt-Keziah briskly took her gun, snapped off the safety and aimed at Keziah.

Then she gunned us down.

I felt several hot streaks pass straight through me, and I doubled up, briefly stabbed by a feeling of raging despair.

But in a few seconds, it passed and I looked up again. Alt-Keziah appeared to be emptying her magazine into Keziah who was standing, unmoved, with her arms folded.

The weapon ran out of ammunition.

Alt-Keziah looked furious. I glanced across at the real Keziah, who, arms folded, was eyeing her back.

'When you go back to your hole,' said the real Keziah. 'You'll find the Bull has gone away as well.'

'Thing is,' said alt-Keziah, 'we nearly took you to the Sump tonight, and we weren't even trying very hard.' She turned to go. 'We didn't need to.' She shouldered her empty weapon and walked away up the path towards the mountains.

'The Bull was deep inside the scar,' I told her. 'I think he uncovered some coffins.'

'My past isn't as easily dug up as it used to be,' said Keziah. 'I'll go bury them. Then I can steer my soul out of here.

# DEREK O'MALLEY

'So,' said Jonah. 'What do we know?'

It was the following night and we all were again at the *Diner*. Normally we don't visit the *Diner* two nights in a row: the broken nights on earth can get to you.

We were reclining in sunloungers around a low table. Jonah lounged in a hammock. Stub sat at a nearby table, under a large umbrella.

'They attacked us as you said they would,' said Keziah.

'They picked on what they thought were our weaknesses,' I said.

'Yes,' replied Jonah.

'But we managed to fight them off. Embarrassing and difficult though it was.'

'Good,' continued Jonah. 'And you visited Michael. What happened?'

'Keziah thought the Scary-Haired Woman had visited him,' I said.

'How can you tell?' asked Corrie.

'The cheap perfume,' replied Keziah. 'But, we think Michael is living a pretty disciplined life and there weren't any signs of damage. In Michael's vegetable garden,' went on Keziah. 'The earth is still very soft but the tunnels are still filled up. So we're cautiously happy.'

'Why, "cautiously?" I asked.

'If he's like a heroin addict, clean and stable is a vulnerable place. You're only one bad day away from disaster.' She shook her head. 'I've known people be clean for months, then go away and inject themselves, just with a normal dose, and their body couldn't take it and they died.'

'You must tire of the relentless cheerfulness of your job,' I said.

'We just think we've got to keep an eye on Michael. He's a dear man but very vulnerable.'

'And Mark?' asked Jonah.

'Jamie and I visited briefly just now while Keziah was having a swim,' said Corrie. 'You give the report, Jamie.'

'Well,' I said. 'He's fine. He's cruising along his happy way.'

I didn't mention the cabin called 'Project K'.

'If I may say something,' said Stub. 'I do think that Vanity Fair's particular weapons are rather blunted against Mr Mark Bright, given his current state of happy optimism.'

'What do you think Vanity Fair will do next?' asked Jonah.

'It's hard to say, sir,' said the evil spirit. 'On the most optimistic scenario, they may do nothing.'

'How does that work?' I asked. 'I thought they were coming under pressure to attack us.'

'Never forget Pandemonium is a bureaucracy. Sir. Somebody gave them orders. They've shown they've tried. The end. Ticky box exercise.'

'We could hope for that,'

'More likely,' said Stub, 'they'll try again.'

'We'll be readier for them next time,' I said. 'More in control.'

'I hope that is indeed the case, sir.'

'One more thing,' added Jonah. 'On top of what Vanity Fair are doing we have your ordinary work. I need to mention Derek O'Malley.

'Aw no!' exclaimed Keziah. 'Not Derek.'

'As you know,' he went on, 'he's in court later this morning and likely to be released from prison.'

I should point out that Cambridge is not Chicago and one dangerous mad person on the streets is (a) plenty (b) noteworthy and (c) likely to be picked up by Keziah. Of the half-dozen firms practicing criminal law in this town, her specialist niche is the Unusually Hopeless. She has it to herself mostly.

'I'm defending him,' she explained. 'He was put in prison a few weeks ago because he pleaded guilty to waving a knife at the warden of his sheltered accommodation. They locked him so they could prepare reports on him.

'Unfortunately he's delusional, aggressive and paranoid. In the three weeks he's been in prison, he's lost his sheltered accommodation and been isolated in the medical wing on one-hour-watch. Prison freaks him out. The report, which has been prepared, says he shouldn't be locked up but he urgently needs a package of care—supervised accommodation and so on.

'But, he's been thrown out of the main place for dangerous mad people in Cambridge and they have to find somewhere else. Which is Social Services' problem. He's also been violent and abusive to the main mental health professional at Social Services. He isn't at the top of her list.'

'So what's going to happen to him today?' I asked.

'I expect we'll let him out of prison onto the streets friendless and totally unsupported.'

'That's appalling,' I said.

'Yes,' said Keziah. 'But on the bright side, your taxes are low. The only real danger is if it all gets too much, he has a bit of a habit of burning buildings down.'

'A bit of a habit of burning buildings down.'

'Yes. Which if he does it again, he'll be in prison forever and who knows what will happen to him.'

'I don't suppose the people in the building will be too keen either. Surely the government will do something?'

'Yeah, good one. Like I said, it's on the desk of Social Services.'

'Social Services have his case on their desk and they're ignoring him?'

'Yes.'

'They knew he was coming out today and they've sat on their hands?'

'Yes.'

'It should be they who are in prison.'

'I used to think that until I saw the pressures they work under.'

I digested this.

'What are we supposed to do?' I asked.

'Sticking plaster job,' said Jonah.

'The idea is we keep him out of trouble,' said Keziah. 'Sooner or later he'll be picked up by a street outreach team or something. If they can find him. I'll talk to Michael as well.'

Keziah finished her smoothie. 'Come on then,' she said to me.

# IT DEPENDS ON THE SAUSAGE

Despite our fears, more weeks then passed. I won't say it was uneventful but it was mostly predictable. We kept doing our sticking plaster jobs on Derek.

On earth, our architects put in a formal application for the conversion of the Strict and Particular Baptist Chapel into a pay-as-you-can cafe and network hub. It would be a cheap-and-cheerful knocking through, stretching our limited start-up budget as far as we could.

If we got takers for the office space in the Chapel and attracted homelessness agencies, we expected the Café to become both a true hub, freed from its constraints at Madge's, and financially self-sustaining.

Mark and Michael schmoozed, reminding local companies of their corporate social responsibility and bending their ears for resources. Their list of contacts was ripening in the sunshine of their persuasion.

They were less successful in persuading government or voluntary agencies to establish a presence in the café. These agencies are slow. But they kept plugging away anyway.

I was busy trying to design some software by which our guests could navigate the available resources and find the help they needed. It needed to be simple, I thought, big screen buttons to jab.

Whenever that project stalled, I worked on the publicity suite for the Cafe.

I was sending the hard coding to my Serbian friend Animal and pushing the design work to Wizzy Graphics, the design shop where my sister Lizzie worked; all my pre-crash freelance buddies.

Mark wanted everything scalable and reproducible. Shoestring budget, small team, lot of talent, big project, it was good fun.

*

Keziah and I were busy many nights, but it seemed we were on top of it. Neither of us were attacked and Michael was OK too.

Mark's soul seemed untroubled. Poignantly, he had fitted a co-pilot's seat on the bridge of his yacht-like soul. It was empty.

So what was happening? Were Vanity Fair plotting? Waiting? Arguing? Panicking?

We had no idea, and Stub did not find any good rumours.

Mark and Keziah were still dating, but so far as I could tell Keziah was forever applying the brakes. She was, I gathered obliquely, hard to pin down and take out anywhere. I wondered whether she was genuinely busy, or like the true workaholic, bingeing on caseload to avoid facing anything like love. Mark could have been forgiven for thinking that Cambridge's destitute had a bigger claim on Keziah than he did.

When I did visit Keziah's soul, however, I noticed that she had moved the pot in which she kept her relationship with Mark. It now had a special place on the moorland of Keziah's soul. The silver birch had grown tall but it was still stuck in its pot. I mentioned none of this to Keziah when we patrolled her soul together, though it was of course, obvious.

I was trying to keep my own mental life in order, and broadly succeeding.

Then there was Derek. I had hardly seen a soul like his: a scrapyard, fires burning, littered with wrecked relationships. Keziah and I visited often, putting fires out, breaking up fights.

On earth we learned Derek had made a nest for himself in the third basement of the multi-storey car park. The police and the street outreach teams both knew this and made sure they never went lower than the second basement.

Derek sometimes came to Madge's when Michael opened the temporary Oyster Café there on Tuesdays and Thursdays.

Michael was trying to find a safe place for Derek and often tried to call social services. The responsible officer was off work for stress.

Nothing very bad, however, had happened.

*

'Developments,' said Kirsty. She was standing on the pavement outside the *Shepherd Diner*. Stub was standing next to her with a chariot ready.

Keziah and I had arrived at the *Diner* almost at the same time. We'd both been summoned by messenger spirits sent to our sleeping heads.

'I was hoping for a meal or something,' I said.

'Bad luck,' said Kirsty. 'Maybe when you get back. Meanwhile, you're going to find out what Vanity Fair are up to next.'

'Where are we going?' I asked.

'We are going to visit the Lady Clemency in Vanity Fair,' said Stub. 'She suggested I brought you.'

'I didn't know we had a friend in Vanity Fair.'

'You'll like her,' said Kirsty.

'I will?'

'Well you ought to,' said Kirsty.

We climbed into the chariot. Stub snapped the reins and we set off.

The evil spirit stood stiff and erect, all seven feet of him, wrapped in his overcoat and with a hat clamped to his head. He hated the golden rain, which had burnt and scarred him over the millennia.

I asked Stub about this Lady Clemency. 'Is she a ride in Vanity Fair?'

'Certainly not, sir. Her home is called "Seasons House" and it is a great provocation to everyone in Vanity Fair and to all of us evil spirits.

'Seasons House has always been in our consciousness, like the golden rain. If the golden rain is like some constant drumming and burning on our skin, Seasons House is more like an intense bright light in our head.

'You have to remember, sir, that we evil spirits have a long history. But the Lady Clemency's is longer.

'She was there from almost the very moment of Creation, when everything was being set up.

'Back in the early days we evil spirits were always making mistakes. You may remember that we once invaded the bodies of the reptiles, thinking they were going to be the dominant lifeform on Earth—'

'That's why you turn into a snake in moments of stress—'

'Indeed, sir, and we got stuck there for 100 million years until a giant asteroid came and ended that age and set us all free.

'Senior colleagues discovered that if you visited Seasons House and stole some of the fruit, you made fewer mistakes.'

'But you said even her presence was painful for you?'

'May I ask if you have ever stolen a hot sausage off a barbecue, sir?'

'I may have,' I said.

'The pain is worth the gain.'

'Depends on the sausage. But point taken.'

'So it became quite normal for us evil spirits to fly into Seasons House, grab something and run off—ah, here's what I want.'

Stub had spotted a dollop of golden rain that was bigger than the *Diner* chariot, falling lazily through the heavens. A floppy, fat disk, it might conceal us from any spying eyes. The *Diner* pengub strained at its leash, tugging our chariot, trying to nibble bits of the blob.

Around us the soul-sucking rides of Vanity Fair twirled enticingly or waved tendrils or reached out with mechanical grabs to harvest the sullen, hungry shoal of human souls that swam among them.

Stub, red eyes gleaming under the brim of a hat, glanced over his shoulder briefly at Keziah and me before focussing again on the pengub and the reins he held.

'You see, sir, I was not, I'm afraid, a very good evil spirit. Have you ever seen a little bird find some food but be pushed off it by a bigger bird? I was subject to quite a bit of bullying.'

'Quite a bit?'

'Over about 13.8 billion years sir.'

'I suppose that would be quite a bit.'

'So in many ways there were easier pickings at Seasons House.

'Cut a long story short, sir, I became a bit of an addict. On wisdom. Which is what grows in Seasons House.'

'On wisdom?'

'Yessir. The Lady Clemency is the Personification of Divine Wisdom.'

'Oh.'

'And I was eating far more than I needed. It started to do strange things to my head. For example, instead of just getting better at my job, I started thinking about leaving my job altogether. I would get terrible thoughts.'

'What kind of terrible thoughts?'

'Obedience. Submission.' Stub shook a little. 'Humility.' He retched. 'Excuse me.'

'No, quite,' I said.

'Handkerchief,' said Keziah, offering him one. Stub wiped his mouth, holding the reins for a moment with a single skeletal hand.

'At the worst I was visiting Seasons House several times a day. I felt sick all the time but kept going back for more.

'I think the word is "flipped" sir. I flipped.'

'Flipped?'

'I defected. Made my way to the *Shepherd Diner* and landed on the pavement outside. I was in my snake-form and suffering convulsions and smoke was rising from my skin. I knew Jonah, of course, he's famous. I offered to work for them. He and Dr Bright nurtured me back to health.'

'And do you still visit Seasons House?'

'Not so much anymore, sir,' said Stub, almost with a trace of pride. 'I've managed to cut down.'

'You've cut down?'

'Yes.'

'What does Jonah think of that?' I said.

'Naturally he disapproves, sir. But I tell him having swapped sides I now want to earn my place in God's favour with my own hands.'

'You believe in God?'

'Of course I believe in God,' snapped Stub. 'All evil spirits believe in God. How can you not believe when there's this laughter echoing round your head all the time? Everything believes in God, fish, birds, trees, everything. Everything except humans. Humans do rather stand out as the most incredibly stupid beings in the Omniverse. My problem, sir, is that I am not sure God believes in me.'

'I thought he'd have a soft spot for a returnee.'

'But He demands perfection.' Stub was moody. 'The most demanding, unyielding, uncompromising Employer in the Universe and I daily betray my former colleagues to try to please him.'

'Stressful.'

'You could say that, sir.'

'You should try atheism. Much easier.'

'Philosophically it is hard to maintain such a foundationless leap of faith,' Stub said, with the air of one who'd tried it.

'I don't mean philosophically. I mean practically. Saves a lot of worry about Eternity.'

Stub looked like he had much more to say, but he had to give attention to the chariot. Keziah and I were silent as we fell past Vanity Fair.

Some rides were like a fairground ghost-train with an entrance and exit; another set were like sea-anenomes that sampled souls as they swung by; yet others resembled Venus fly-traps that swallowed souls whole for a while, before spitting them out, bleached and pitted.

'These souls are being feasted on,' I said. 'And none of them know.'

'With respect sir,' said Stub, pulling on the reins to steer us around a ride that was squirting a kind of ink into the heavens. 'I think they all know.'

'How do you mean?'

'They all know sir. When they gossip, or get cynical, or gamble, or hate, or lust or worry or despise themselves. They all know there's a transaction going on in their souls. They know they're feeding something. But they ignore the feelings and put their minds to something else.'

'We could work here for years and not make a dent.'

'Fortunately you are not the only players, sir. Here is our destination. Seasons House.'

I looked around me. 'Good grief. It's vast.'

# SEASONS HOUSE

Swinging into view was a truly enormous square building, miles wide, like an insanely-scaled pergola or Greek temple. It was towed through the heavens by a flock of pengubim. I counted seven pillars on each side. Giant trees and flowers grew inside it. Fountains played. Climbing plants coiled around the pillars, heavy with blossom or fruit.

Many souls played here. Some swooped into the fountains, washing themselves in the gold-shining spray. Others burrowed into flowers, seeking pollen or perfume. Others again navigated through tree branches, getting showered with blossom as they passed through. Some of the fruit was gold or silver. Music played.

Stub steered our chariot between two of the pillars and after a long pull, set us down in a meadow whose grass brushed halfway up our wheels and was speckled with wildflowers. We clambered off the chariot and looked around.

A river flowed nearby. Butterflies flapped and swooped. Trees dotted the fields. Far beyond, dimmed by distance and heat-haze, stood the yellowy stone pillars that formed the edges of Seasons House.

'What do we do now?' I asked.

'Help yourself to some fruit or nuts, I would suggest,' said Stub. 'The Lady Clemency will be here in a minute.'

'Who is she exactly?'

'Think about it sir,' said Stub. 'Here in the middle of Vanity Fair. Amid the greed, the addiction, the compulsions, the empty pleasure-seeking. Massive, open on all sides, filled with fruit for anyone to take. The heavens are always mixed, sir.'

'Wisdom,' said a new voice. 'The Lady Wisdom is my official title. Call me Clemency.'

I spun round.

'Morning,' she said. Clemency was one of those lean, crinkly-eyed, difficult-to-age women, taller than me, with straight grey hair cut short, short linen jacket and jeans. She had tiny emerald ear-studs, a prominent nose and a slightly crooked smile. Her head was slightly to one side, weighing us up. Her black eyes smoked with intelligence, hard to look at.

Stub took off his hat, and twirling it in his hands, briefly introduced us and our story. He would not meet her gaze.

'I've seen you here, Keziah,' said Clemency. 'And Jamie, I think you've occasionally stumbled through.'

'Yeah,' I said breezily. 'Feels very familiar. But probably I could come more.'

'Probably you could,' said Clemency, slightly distantly. 'Let's sit down.'

She led us over a little bridge to a shady tree under which were some garden chairs and a table. We took our seats. One of Clemency's interns brought some tea and Clemency poured.

'This sound,' she said, as the tea splashed into a cup, 'destroys empires. Shortbread?'

After we'd all been supplied, she continued. 'You work with Jonah and Corrie Bright. We're in the same business but we subvert from below.'

'How does that work, then?' I asked, not keeping up at all.

'Even your most blind, self-destructive spirit needs wisdom. They have to come.'

'Even the demons must come,' said Stub.

'Right,' said Clemency. 'They hate it, but they can't work without it.'

'And you don't mind?' I asked.

'Course not,' said Clemency. 'Subverting the subversive. Didn't do you any harm Stub?'

'I do not know, my lady,' said Stub.

'You don't eat enough, that's the problem.'

'I find I can't keep it down, my lady.'

'Anyway,' said Clemency. 'Your position is this. You were recruited to a soul-fixing team and caused a level of irritation to the local satanic hierarchy.

'Then Mark Bright comes along.' Clemency cast a brief look at Keziah before carrying on. 'The Universe resonates when he speaks. Down in the hierarchy are research departments which look for this kind of person. Up come the orders to Vanity Fair to stop Mark.'

'And Vanity Fair came to you for advice,' said Keziah.

'No. They trusted their instincts first,' said Clemency. 'Now that that has failed, they're on their way.'

'What, now?' I said.

'Yes,' said Clemency. 'I thought you'd enjoy watching.

# AN AUDIENCE WITH THE LADY WISDOM

Clemency pointed at the tree in whose shade we were sitting. 'Hollow,' she said. 'It's old-tech but it's served eavesdroppers for hundreds of years.'

She opened a door in the tree trunk and ushered us in. Inside the hollow tree were a couple of stools, along with a small table containing bowls of fruit and some glasses of drink. Spy-holes were conveniently placed so you could sit on the stools and look out. Keziah and I took one each. Stub led the *Diner* chariot and pengub to another part of Seasons House.

We settled ourselves and watched Clemency's interns clear our leavings away and put out a chair for the Scary-Haired Woman, some straw for the Bull, and lay a dog-bed for the Black Dog. Two interns carried over a large sandpit for the Sphinx, set it down and smoothed the sand with a plank.

Clemency meanwhile took her seat, her back straight, the calm poise of the effortless aristocrat.

The leaders of Vanity Fair arrived by what looked like a hot air balloon, except for the Sphinx, who flew alongside with heavy beats of its dragon wings. It landed in its sandpit, nodded briefly at Clemency, folded its ebony body and yawned. The hot air balloon slightly overshot, and didn't land smoothly, and the gate in the basket jammed, but eventually the Bull, the

Black Dog and the Woman with all the arms arrived and took their places.

'You asked to see me and you're very welcome,' said Clemency. 'How may I help?'

There was a silence, apart from the slobbering noises of the Black Dog nosing the bowl against the forest floor. The Sphinx turned his face away from him.

'We find,' said the Sphinx, 'that we are having to dirty our hands with jobs that are rather beneath us.'

'It makes me so mad,' moaned the Bull, looking up from his hay. 'It's like, extra work, no consultation, no compensation. What are we supposed to do, just do it?'

'None of that's true,' growled the Black Dog. 'Fact is, we're stuffed. Totally out of our depth. A dog chew might relieve the gloom.'

The intern rummaged through her trolley and threw him one.

'I prefer to think of it as beneath me rather than beyond me,' sniffed the Sphinx.

'It just makes me so mad,' said the Bull.

Clemency held up a hand. 'As I understand it, those further along the management hierarchy—'

'Entirely out of touch,' sneered the Sphinx. 'Haven't done proper work for centuries.'

'I just want to charge something,' muttered the Bull. 'Charge and gore.'

'And who are you going to stick your horns into? Our bosses?' asked the Sphinx. 'Good plan.'

'Quite,' said Clemency. 'They've asked you to work with a small network of people gathered around the social entrepreneur Mark Bright, who lives in the region covered by your part of Vanity Fair.'

'And he's totally incorruptible,' muttered the Scary-Haired Woman with all the arms. She downed a cocktail. 'Teflon. And we haven't had any success with the others.'

'Losing your touch, sweetheart,' said the Black Dog, who then with a large retch threw up the contents of his stomach. 'Processed food,' he grunted approvingly, and set to eating it again.

The Scary Haired Woman tossed her head and snarled with her black teeth. 'If you'd seen the list of my victims, you wouldn't use words like "*losing my touch.*" And the driven types like Mark are usually easy. Just make them equally driven in their secret life. But I put an idea in Mark's head and he just flicks it off.'

'Not depressed, that's the problem. That's what you need.'

'And you've been no help.'

'Nothing to get my teeth into, chocolate-chops. Can't help you. Bowl of fresh water would be nice by the way.'

The intern obliged.

'If I may,' said Clemency, with another perfectly judged cough. 'Perhaps it's better to see all this in a slightly wider framework. You have indeed been asked to do special work beyond the normal.'

'Not what I signed up for,' bellowed the Bull.

'We didn't sign up for anything,' snapped the Scary Haired Woman. 'If you remember we seized power in a coup.'

'Still,' grumbled the Bull, 'natural justice. Common law.'

'Always was going to go pear-shaped,' observed the Dog, muzzle dripping.

'Oh, the tedium of working with micro-minds,' mused the Sphinx.

'My point is,' said Clemency, 'there is a reward for succeeding.'

'Allegedly,' said the Black Dog.

'But unlikely to amount to anything substantive,' added the Sphinx.

'And trouble is,' said the Black Dog, 'even if you do succeed, and get a reward, what happens then? What happens? More damned for eternity, that's what happens.'

There was a silence.

'Gotta say it how it is,' rasped the Dog. 'Cruel, but there you are.'

'I understand there's also a punishment for failing,' added Clemency.

'Which is temporary, which means immediate. Which is like, straightaway,' reasoned the Dog. 'I wouldn't totally object to a belly rub, by the way.'

The intern obliged, but even that didn't seem to dislodge the gloom that was spreading among the four beasts, and the Dog shook her off and scratched his ear with his back leg. 'Damned if we succeed. Punished if we fail. Stuffed if we do nothing,' he growled. 'And we're totally out of our depth. Part from that, everything's fine.'

'Have you thought of hiring a consultant?' asked Clemency.

'This lot wouldn't think of anything,' said the Black Dog. 'They just go for the reptile parts of people's minds, you know, the basic urges. Not like depression which needs proper intellect.'

'You haven't a clue,' said the Scary Haired Woman. 'You just haven't a clue.'

'My idea,' resumed Clemency, 'is this. You hire a consultant. He's responsible for coordinating the attacks on Mark and his network. If he succeeds, he gets the rewards.'

'But gets even more punishment in eternity,' said the Black Dog.

'And if he fails,' continued Clemency, 'he takes the blame. Either way, you are seen to have acted, and you've outsourced the problem.'

The four beasts considered this.

'Not only so,' said Clemency, 'but you may be adding a fresh depth of expertise and subtlety to your efforts.'

'I see a problem,' said the Black Dog. 'Where do you get one of these consultants?'

'That's not as hard as you'd imagine,' said Clemency. 'All you've got to do is find a spirit with a different make-up from yourselves. For example, someone whose pride and vanity makes them think they can succeed where all others fail.'

'But he'll still get toasted in eternity,' said the Black Dog, 'more than us even.'

'I wish you'd stop going on about that,' said the Bull. 'Makes me so mad.'

'Fact of eternal life,' said the Dog.

'Merely a fairy tale,' sneered the Sphinx. 'A leap of faith.'

'Wait and see, Catface,' insisted the Dog.

'Nevertheless,' said Clemency, 'even if it's true, and even if your consultant believes it's true, the thought might not stop him. While he's—as you say—*toasting*, he will comfort himself with the thought that he lived a brilliant life. Like a shiny meteor, he streaked across the sky. Live bright and burn, but at least live.'

'That does work,' said the Scary Haired Woman. 'I use that a lot.'

'I still don't see where you would get him,' said the Black Dog.

'I do,' said Clemency. 'Find someone who hates his present job and thinks it's beneath him. Somebody who has tried before to make a name for himself and failed. Someone convinced of his own brilliance. And ideally, someone local to the Cambridge scene.'

At this point, Keziah tapped me with her foot. I withdrew from the peephole and looked at her.

'What?' I mouthed.

'Leopold,' she mouthed back.

I thought for a moment. 'Leopold.'

# LEOPOLD

A few days later Stub, who spies on these things for us, confirmed that Leopold Xavier Squamata St Germain, evil spirit, formerly of the Complaints Department in Pandemonium, and before that the being who had kidnapped us and experimented on us, had been appointed as a consultant to Vanity Fair.

It was a perfect afternoon at the *Diner* for our weekly meeting. Down on earth it was the grumpy, low, mid-part of the night, realm of angry insomniacs and nurses on one night-shift too many.

Warm breezes wafted us, impelled by a lazy ceiling fan. Keziah and I were wet-haired and refreshed from a swim, though we had changed back to our ordinary clothes. Kirsty had mixed large drinks and laid out salty snacks and fresh fruit. Corrie, Jonah and Stub joined us. Jonah had taken to his hammock between two palm trees; the rest of us sat round a table by the pool.

On the agenda: if Vanity Fair was honing its attack by hiring Leopold, we needed to prepare our defences.

'I can't understand why The Lady Clemency advised them to recruit Leopold,' I complained.

'It was the wise thing to do,' said Keziah.

'But it doesn't help us.'

'So tipping us off was also the wise thing to do,' said Keziah. 'It's not difficult.'

'We need to think about Leopold's strategy,' said Corrie Bright. 'Keziah?'

I didn't mind Corrie turning to Keziah for this contribution. When it comes to dark plotting, she would be my go-to.

'What are his main qualities?' she asked aloud. 'He's vain. He believes he's superior to any being in the heavens. He's ambitious: he wants to get prizes and accolades.'

'He is smart,' I added. 'He can make long-term plans, he can be patient, he can be cunning and deceitful. He went to a lot of bother to get hold of us the first time.'

'But like all evil spirits he also loves the reptile way of just butchering human souls and feasting on the offal. Which curbs his patience. Alright. So here's Leopold, newly promoted and ready for action. What is his long-term goal?' asked Keziah.

'Easy,' I said. 'He wants to put me, you, Michael and Mark into the Sump of Lost Dreams where he feasts on us until he's crunched the last bone. Ideally, he'd like to be put back in charge of Vanity Fair and win prizes and be famous. And perhaps produce a course for other evil spirits that he can deliver across the heavens.'

'But will he want the Oyster Café to succeed or fail?' asked Jonah, whom I thought was asleep.

'He wants it to fail. That's what he's been hired for,' I said.

'Not necessarily,' said Keziah, warming to the discussion now that it was about wolverine cunning and perfidy. 'If the Oyster Café got started, but was run by a team of people who were—I dunno—divided, hypocritical, disillusioned, it could be even more successful for Pandemonium than if it failed.'

This conversation was getting a bit beyond me.

'So you're saying the Café could be a failure, or it could succeed and be a still bigger failure?'

'That's right,' said Keziah. 'A notionally do-gooding operation consumed by cynicism or frustrated ambition. Nice.'

'So we have to ask ourselves whether Leopold wants the Café to fail obviously and publicly, setting Mark back, or to succeed, but on Leopold's terms,' suggested Corrie.

'Except,' said Keziah, animated now, 'Leopold's not a totally free actor. He's been hired. You know what Vanity Fair's like. He'll have performance management targets. He'll need to meet certain criteria along the way so he doesn't get fired.'

'Such as what?' I asked.

'Stop the Oyster Café. Make it not happen. That would be measurable. And short-term enough for his bosses.'

'So we *do* think he's trying to stop the Oyster Café,' I said.

'Probably,' said Keziah. 'So here's what he'll do. First he'll gather information. He can do that, can't he Stub?'

'Yes miss,' said the evil spirit. 'Plenty of spirits make a living collecting data. He can either bribe or torture them, whichever works best.'

'Then he makes plans. And we can expect him to be subtle and more imaginative and more wide ranging than the Vanity Fair folks.'

'In which case I have an idea,' I said.

'You do?'

'Yes. *Yes.* I, Jamie, have an idea.'

'Well we'd better hear it,' said Corrie in the short silence that followed.

'Mark thinks there's something going on at Planning. He keeps calling. But it depends totally on who answers the phone. (When the phone is actually answered.) One time they'll say it's impossible and give you a long list of reasons why the plans are going to be turned down. Another time they'll tell you, sounds reasonable, shouldn't be a problem. The only official meeting we had was negative. And we're waiting for a decision. Mark thinks we're caught up in some war between the planning officers.'

'Which is perfect for Leopold,' said Corrie. 'If there's pre-existing bitterness and rivalry he's got plenty to work with.'

'And it would be a whole area of attack on the Oyster Café that we weren't prepared for,' I said.

'Except I was saying that weeks ago,' said Keziah.

'Problem is, it wasn't true then,' I said. 'But it is now.'

'So,' said Corrie. 'Jobs. Kirsty needs to keep interrogating the gossip networks. Find out what's happening on earth. Look at the planning department.'

'More socializing in Gossiper Space,' said Kirsty, referring to that perpetual lunch-break in the heavens where the gossipers networked with each other. 'Has to be done.'

'I'm also willing to visit Gossiper Space,' I said. 'If needed.'

'Noted,' said Jonah from his hammock.

'Stub can keep spying on the evil spirits,' continued Corrie.

'I hope I give satisfaction, Ma'am,' said Stub.

'And the rest of us?' I asked. 'I get it. We have to be prepared for subtle random attacks from any direction.'

# JULIAN FABER, MASTER PLANNER

All the dimensions of the heavens exist alongside each other. But that is too much for the poor brains of most of us to cope with, so we view the heavens through filters. Via the normal filter, called Enhanced Soul Space, we can visualize souls and spirits and many of the other influences that act on souls.

Also taking up a lot of room in Enhanced Soul Space is the Department, the civil service of the heavenlies, who like to think they organize everything. They police the laws of physics, and design snowflakes and weather systems, for example.

Other dimensions of the heavenlies exist alongside Enhanced Soul Space. The Noetic Realm of Maths, for example, contains the source code for all pure mathematics throughout the Universe. Corrie Bright, I am told, goes surfing there but I have never visited that fractured realm, where sets of axioms elementally grind against each other.

Keziah and I have additionally spent time at the School of Ideas, viewable through still another filter, where ideas meet, play, reshape themselves, and return to their host souls. Corrie and Jonah are often found in a higher but linked dimension, the University of Metanarratives.

Heaven's research library is accessed through still another filter called Gossiper Space. This is Kirsty's natural habitat. All the beings who clean and maintain the heavens—the gossipers—gather here to share news about the universe. It's vastly hospitable, and visiting it would be one of my favourite assignments: no piece of information, however obscure, is further than six meals away.

*

Kirsty, however, rather than sending us to Gossiper Space to find out about the Planning Department, merely contacted us one early morning a few days later. We rode up to the *Diner*.

'You were right,' she told us.

'I was?' I said. 'I was hoping to get a decent meal out of the research.'

'I thought I served you decent meals,' said Kirsty.

'You do,' I said hastily. 'Marvellous. Wonderful meals. Who would want anything else? You said you could help.'

'I *could*,' said Kirsty. 'But if people start insulting my cooking.'

'No, no,' I insisted. 'Of course... I mean who would... remarkable...'

Satisfied I was now fully deflated, Kirsty continued. 'The Planning Department: the person who gave Mark the initial advice is called Julian Faber. He's the one who's now received the formal plans.

'He's going to reject them, and he's made a list of reasons already. The plans are still sitting on his desk because he wants it to look like they've been properly considered.'

'Have they been properly considered?' I asked.

'Of course not,' said Kirsty. 'There aren't enough planners any more for that kind of thing.'

'Why is he rejecting the plans?'

'Politics. He believes the state should look after the needy, and not contract it out to charities who are probably funded by big business for their own evil ends and fronted by people who believe in fairies at the bottom of the garden.'

'He doesn't like Michael's dog collar,' I said.

'However, there's a senior planner in the department. His name's Colin Studd. He's guessed what Julian is doing.'

'And he's going to act.'

'Maybe,' said Kirsty. 'His job is also to give the junior planners responsibility. Sometimes that means letting them make wrong decisions.

'Add to that: Colin hates conflict, he's not decisive, he's totally overburdened and he's not lightning fast at his job. So quite a lot happens in Planning because Colin dithers too long to stop it.

'You want more? He doesn't like Julian at all, in fact he'd like to wring his neck. But *that* means he's *oversensitive* to micro-managing him, so he tends to let Julian get away with decisions that are wrong.'

Corrie and Keziah allowed a lengthy pause while I slotted this together in my head.

'I see,' I said eventually, hoping I did. 'And how does this all affect us?'

'It's coming to a head. I suggest you visit Colin's soul around 12 noon on Friday. He has to act this week.'

'Why that time?'

'Three hours to answer his emails, sharpen his pencils and practice all his other dithering strategies. Twelve o'clock because that's only an hour till lunch and he's away all afternoon. He'll have to do it then.'

'I'm not in court tomorrow,' said Keziah. 'I could block out that hour.'

'Yeah, and I think I'll be the only one in our office so I should be alright too,' I said. I could doze in front of my computer and no-one would know the difference.

'Good,' said Corrie.

'Has Stub got anywhere spying on Leopold?'

'Not very far,' said Corrie. 'Leopold acts alone and keeps everything secret. But if he's been collecting information like we have, he will know that tomorrow is the time to go and visit Julian.'

# TRACTORIZED

Friday. I started work. I had got into the bad habit of checking my social networks before setting out on the main business of the day.

One message stood out among the screenfuls of red-eyed partygoers and baby photos.

Lottie, who since her move to Mexico with new husband Umberto had been very quiet, had updated her status.

*I have returned from Mexico and am staying with my mum in Lincolnshire. Umberto is in prison in Mexico. He is facing charges of domestic abuse and battery. I will be divorcing him as soon as UK law allows. I will not be putting up further posts and would be grateful if you didn't contact me. I will not be visiting this page again. Thanks.*

I read the message many times. I needed to, because I was using it to move heavy furniture around in my head.

*Lottie and Umberto are no more.*
*That didn't last very long.*
*Lottie is back in England.*

It wasn't so much moving mental furniture as wandering round some ancient chateau-of-the-mind, pulling dust covers off sofas, and opening old shutters onto broad horizons.

I needed to talk to someone.

I poked my speed dial.

'Lizzie,' I said to my sister.

'Oove een a oose?'

'Lizzie, take the pencil out of your mouth.'

'Sorry. You've seen the news?' she said.

'Lottie is back. Have you heard anything else?'

'No.'

'Me neither. I need to go see her.'

'What?'

'I need to go see her. We all do. The old crew.'

'I thought her post said don't contact her?'

'She obviously didn't mean us.'

'No, Jamie. She might be … wounded or something.'

'No, I'm sure that message is for the, you know, public. Not for her real friends.'

'I think she means everybody Jamie. Including us.'

'We could cheer her up.'

'Jamie.' There was a pause. I could imagine Lizzie at the other end trying to arrange some words in her head. This is not easy when you are as dyslexic as she is, not knowing her right from her left, or indeed, her right from her wrong. Lizzie's general approach to words of more than two syllables was to dash at them and hope for the best. 'You can't … she might be … this might take a while.'

'Yes, but we can speed it up.'

'No. I just think—'

'That's ridiculous. It's the perfect thing. We could go up, take her out of herself.'

'I think you should wait for her to get in touch with us.'

'But what if she doesn't?'

'She will.'

'But how long will that take?'

'I don't know. Months. A year. I don't know—'

'A *year*?'

'Well I don't know. But she's obviously tractorized.'

'Traumatized.'

'That's what I said.'

'So you're suggesting we sit around for a year, doing nothing, with Lottie two hours up the road? You're not being very helpful Lizzie.'

'I'm trying to think of things from her point of view.'

'Yes but people get … self-absorbed.'

'Do they.'

'Yes. So I was thinking, what's the harm in just phoning her up?'

'Don't.'

My sister has the personality type normally referred to in internet dating sites as 'bubbly,' which is usually (as it is in Lizzie's case) a synonym for 'airhead.' But she sounded unusually sure of herself and serious. And if she doesn't have at least emotional intelligence, I thought to myself, what kind does she have? It certainly doesn't extend to spelling. Or balancing a budget. Or cooking. Or counting units of alcohol.

'I suppose I could wait a week,' I said. 'Let her get over the jet lag.'

My heart was thumping.

But it was nearly 12 by now, and my spirit was needed on the soul of Cambridge City Council's senior planner.

# THE WAR ON COLIN STUDD'S SOUL (PART ONE)

The soul of Colin Studd, senior planner, was a dumpy cargo vessel, overloaded, top-heavy, knee-deep with stuff.

Keziah and I landed cautiously on the corner of his deck and climbed out of our chariot. Down on earth, presumably, Colin was at his desk, looking over at Julian, twiddling with his pencil, and reflecting that it was Friday, and he just had to talk to Julian about the Strict and Particular Baptist Chapel application.

It was unlikely that anyone would spot us here. The deck of Colin's soul was piled high: children's paintings and junk models. Rolls of wallpaper and a pasting table. Broken toys needing mending. A lawnmower, a rake and a hedge-trimmer. A pile of washing up. A half-built model trireme, made of lollipop sticks, the sort of homework project that cruel junior schoolteachers inflict not so much on their students as on their students' parents. A stepladder. A sponge and bucket with which to wash his car. Mounds of paper. Flapping things tumbled from the sky like falling blossom.

I picked one of them up. 'Thank you for contacting the Bank yesterday,' it squawked. 'Could you fill in a five-minute feedback form?'

I pulled its head off, but more kept coming.

'Will you stop messing about?' said Keziah.

'It's like being stuck in a to-do list,' I said. 'His whole soul is a to-do list.'

'Shush. Look!'

The steering wheel on Colin's soul was open to the elements. Colin was standing at his wheel, a rumpled, donnish man in mid-life.

A being was talking to him. This tall being was also no longer young, despite his jeans, his amber perma-tan, and his ponytail.

'There he is!' I hissed. 'I was right!'

Leopold.

'Come on,' said Keziah, and we scuttled between the piles of stuff to get nearer, like First World War soldiers in trenches.

'What are you going to do?' I whispered.

'What do you think?' hissed Keziah. 'Argue.'

'Why?' I asked. 'We'll give ourselves away.'

'What do you want me to do?' hissed Keziah back. 'Sit back while Leopold does whatever he likes?'

'I dunno. Watch. Plan. Think. I don't know.'

Keziah started climbing up a pile of old magazines until she was in full view.

'You see, Colin,' Leopold was saying, 'Julian may make mistakes. But he is developing. If he gets the odd project wrong, well, it makes him a better planner in the long term.'

Leopold suddenly saw Keziah and his face tightened.

'On the other hand,' interrupted Keziah, 'No project should be improperly or unjustly turned down.'

For a moment, Leopold turned ash-grey. A long tongue flicked out of his mouth. With a twitch he forcibly returned himself back to his tanned colour and withdrew the tongue. He turned back to Colin and resumed his casual drawl. 'Everything is appealable, Colin. So you can give Julian plenty of rope.'

'There is no excuse for wrong and ludicrous decisions *ever* to come from a department that you manage, Colin,' said Keziah.

'Oh I don't know,' said Colin, to himself, (sitting at his desk he thought he was merely thinking to himself while he twiddled with his pencil). 'Why change the habit of a lifetime?'

'Heavy-handed management,' returned Leopold, 'will just make a headstrong person more headstrong. The way Julian will learn best is by being given his head, and yes, tasting failure.'

'I think, Colin,' said Keziah, watching Leopold like he was a poisonous snake, 'this isn't about techniques for helping Julian develop. It's about whether you are willing to confront him.'

'Oh dear,' said Colin.

'And how many innocent people have to suffer by having promising planning applications refused?'

'Manage Julian too harshly and you could lose him,' Leopold countered.

'Good,' said Keziah.

'Hmm,' mused Colin, 'would solve a few problems.'

'Don't forget the ban on hiring,' said Leopold. 'There's no replacing him.'

'Oh dear, dear,' said Colin.

'What will your wife think if you have to do still longer hours?' said Leopold.

'Fundamentally,' insisted Keziah steadily, 'it's about running the department right and doing the job right. You can't have a junior planner behaving like Stalin. What are you paid for?'

I could see Colin's hands gripping his ship's wheel tightly.

'I have to do it,' he whispered to himself. 'I have to confront him.'

'Do it next week,' suggested Leopold, lazily, his amiable tone contrasting with the venomous eyes that he kept on Keziah. 'There's no hurry.'

'I have to do it today.'

'You need coffee first,' suggested Leopold.

'I'll need coffee afterwards,' said Colin. 'And I'll deserve it.'

'All you've got to do,' said Keziah, with a surprising softness in her voice, not a tone I'd ever heard when she spoke to me, 'is just amble over to Julian and say, "Ah, that file about the Baptist Chapel on Mill Road—I think I'll just run my eyes over it, if that's OK. We can have a chat later. See if we both agree."'

Leopold was twitching but couldn't seem to think of anything to say.

'There's a couple of emails you must do first,' Leopold finally spluttered. 'And then you can have an early lunch.'

'Nope,' said Colin. 'Get it over with.' He turned his ship's wheel sharply, tied it in place, and then disappeared down some steps.

Keziah and Leopold looked at each other.

'Mordant!' Leopold spat.

'Good morning.'

'I heard you were working for Jonah and Corrie Bright. And Jamie as well? Or has he chickened out?'

'No, I'm here,' I said, putting my head over the junk and waving. 'I was just—er—covering her back.'

'Ill-judged and unwise,' said Leopold, ignoring me. 'You don't know what you are taking on.'

'You do, though, Leopold,' returned Keziah evenly.

'You are bad news, Mordant,' said Leopold. 'And it will not end well for you.'

'And you've had an unbroken run of success since we last met. How was the Complaints Department?'

Leopold twitched violently. 'I have a war to win. And I do not need to stay here to do it.'

He sprouted a pair of reptile wings, and with heavy beats, flew away.

We watched him go.

'One-nil,' I said.

'Maybe,' said Keziah. 'Anyway, Colin has taking over the planning decision. This is good. And I've gotta get back to the office.'

'Busy?'

'Well I'm seeing someone at lunchtime. I'm trying to get him interested in Derek O'Malley.'

'Your arsonist friend. Where is he?'

'Still in the third basement of the car park.'

'It's not really your job though, is it?'

'He's *our* job actually. And keeping him out of prison is definitely my job.'

# THE WAR ON COLIN STUDD'S SOUL (PART TWO)

It wasn't right that no-one was welcoming Lottie home: over the coming days the thought began to nag at me.

Chocolate shops in the tourist town of Cambridge have made the happy discovery that however expensive and exclusive the current market leader, room exists for one further up the scale.

The current alpha chocolate shop had more than a hint of an expensive jewellers, carpets, subtle lighting, white-gloved assistants, and tiny dark chocolates resting in individual paper baskets in glass-fronted cabinets that you could slide open.

Women wandered blankly around the shop, sometimes dragging boyfriends, not buying anything, just in a daze of lust.

I took a small box, and navigating carefully around the zombie women, selected six fine chocolates for Lottie. Stem ginger. Chilli. Truffle. That kind of thing. At the counter I asked for a mailing box and handed over £24 for the chocolates plus some more for the mailing box. A girl took my money and passed the chocolates to her manager, who wrapped the chocolates, tied a ribbon, then slid them neatly into the mailing box. I had already thought about the gift label and settled for a simple ♡ *Jamie*.

You can't do a short trip to the Post Office—because it's the Post Office—but after a long trip to the Post Office the job was done.

*

When I got home that night I was fiddling with my key in the door when I heard the voice of a messenger spirit in my head.

'You're needed, lad.'

'I haven't time!' I snapped.

'It's an emergency,' said the messenger spirit (a no-nonsense type called Leonard). 'And you aren't doing anything anyway.'

I let myself into the house, and after a moment's thought, headed into the bathroom and locked the door. My sister Lizzie wasn't back yet from Wizzy Graphics but if she did turn up, she knew I spent ages in the loo. I flipped myself up to the heavens.

Kirsty gave us a quick report. Colin had indeed taken the Oyster Cafe file from Julian. He'd read through it, decided it should be approved, and compiled a list of reasons.

He'd then heard Julian's reasons to turn it down. Julian's real reason was that he didn't like turning over social problems to charities and God-botherers. But his official reason was that the Oyster Café would fill Mill Road with street people, who'd be begging and drinking in the streets.

Colin reasoned the opposite: the Oyster Cafe was excellent provision for the poor, a good facility for the whole city. As for Mill Road, laws against street drinking and begging were already in place.

He had then, according to Kirsty, simply said, 'I think, Julian, I should take this one over. I've just had

120

an application for a new development of social housing on a former pub site. I'll swap that one with you.'

Julian Faber had not liked this at all. All in one conversation, their disagreement had grown up, married, and had children. Soon Julian was channelling his inner shop steward and had started introducing phrases like 'bullying', 'harassment', 'Employment Tribunal.'

Colin had held his ground, all the time sinking deeper into gloom. And the atmosphere in the office hissed with sulphur.

The traffic jam that Colin had then driven into that evening—and where he was currently embedded—was one of Cambridge's finest, a solid seam of stationary metal that only narrowly escaped becoming an actual geological feature.

Colin's car audio was not working. He was left with nothing to do but gaze at the back of a supermarket delivery van.

'So Colin's stuck in a traffic jam, very fed up, hating the conflict,' concluded Kirsty, after describing all this. 'Leopold's probably furious. So it might be a good idea to visit Colin again.'

*

'What are we going to do?' I whispered to Keziah as we crouched behind a barricade of several years' worth of half-read copies of the *Town and Country Planners' Journal* that had accumulated on Colin's soul.

'Watch and wait.'

Above Colin's soul, the heavens were purplish, streaked with contrails, complex with rides and souls.

'I don't see Leopold arguing with him,' I said.

'Look over there,' said Keziah. 'Do you think the sky's getting dark?'

'Possibly.' I could see a dark mass growing in the distance.

'What do you think that is?'

'I've no idea.'

We heard a buzzing noise as the cloud got nearer.

'That cloud ... they're all individual beings,' I said. 'With tools. Or weapons.'

'He's sent an army,' said Keziah.

I looked at her. Her chalk-white face was thoughtful. 'You don't think we should run away or something.'

'Nope.'

'I mean obviously to get help and then come back.'

'Nope.'

The Black Dog emerged out of the cloud and landed. He was facing Colin on the prow of his ship. Colin was holding his ship's wheel and we were concealed in the clutter behind him.

The Dog stiffened all four paws into the debris, tossed back his head, and howled. Then he howled again.

I felt my mood sink. 'It's an *army*,' I said.

'Discouragement is what the Dog does,' said Keziah. 'Get a grip.'

'Sometimes discouragement is a rational response to discouraging events,' I muttered.

'C'mon boys!' yelled the Black Dog. 'And the females too,' he said, 'of course. Gotta have the females.'

Colin sighed. He did look like all the problems of the world had just tumbled out of a wet paper bag above his head.

A pack of dog-like creatures emerged from the cloud, landed on Colin's soul, and started sniffing. Then, all over his ship, they started crouching down and leaving doggy deposits.

'No, no, no!' exclaimed Colin, as if suddenly overwhelmed by discouragements all around.

One bulldog-like being put its nose round our barricade.

'Get away,' I hissed. 'Go on, off!'

Slightly puzzled, the dog slunk away.

'Nice job everybody,' rasped the Black Dog after a few minutes. 'Walkies! Home now!'

The dogs turned and scurried back to the prow and jumped off.

This took a few moments because some of the dogs stopped to sniff interesting things, or to finish their toilet.

It began to rain, a drizzle first, then quickly a full downpour. The rain sparkled and glistened as it fell and seemed to sink into Colin's soul.

We next heard the heavy beat of wings. The Sphinx appeared and lowered itself carefully on the deck, looking round to avoid all the dog poo. It raised its head and looked Colin calmly in the face.

'See what Leopold's doing,' said Keziah. 'Soften Colin up with gloom. Then bring on the head of the Sneering Group.'

'The whole system is falling apart, Colin,' the Sphinx said smoothly, grimacing because of the rain. 'Budget cuts, poor management, low calibre of trainee, political pressure, greedy developers with deep pockets. A good man like you is totally outgunned. Colin. The people suffer. Nothing you can do.

'A fair, just, balanced, equable planning system? It's gone, Colin.'

Colin's shoulders slumped. He looked like some sort of wounded antelope about to be finished off with a spear.

'Julian Faber? Totally unreasonable. Out of control. And are you given the resources to manage him properly? You are not. You are left on your own and then blamed for his excesses. Lose-lose arrangement Colin. Cambridge loses. The planning system loses, and you lose.'

As we watched, a young woman landed gently next to the Sphinx—also avoiding the dog poo. Pretty, shy, looking down, she trod between the junk—out of our view for a moment—then appeared at the top of the stairs, on Colin's open-air bridge.

'Who's that' I asked Keziah.

'Look at the teeth,' Keziah whispered back.

Tentatively, the young woman reached out and momentarily brushed Colin's hand with her fingers. Both his hands were still clinging tightly to his ship's wheel.

Everyone was getting drenched.

She smiled.

Colin eyed her.

'Colin!' she whispered. 'That Baptist Chapel. Prime land—you know that. Prime building land. Why should it go to this penniless charity? It doesn't have to. Colin!

'You could get a nicer house. Maybe one of those large Victorian terraces in Granchester Meadows, one of the Ten Best Locations in Britain. A planner's dream. You've fought the flow long enough, Colin dear. It's time to go with it. A top planner like you can make a lot of money, escape from all this.'

She smiled wider, but this time it was spoilt a little by the glimpse of black teeth.

'Traffic's still jammed,' oozed the Sphinx. 'We'll all be here for hours.'

The woman walked up to him, cusped her hand and whispered something in his ear.

'Bribes,' said Colin.

The woman stepped back and looked wide-eyed at him.

'No, no no,' she said. 'Using your brain to leverage legitimate financial opportunities. And improving the cityscape at the same time. Reject certain plans. Smooth the path for someone else. Perhaps receive a discreet thank-you. Everybody wins.'

'I see,' said Colin.

'Everybody wins,' repeated the woman.

'Hmm,' said Colin.

'We're stuffed,' I whispered to Keziah. 'Everything they've said is true.' She seemed to be feeling the gloom too.

Colin left his steering wheel. 'Would you be kind enough just to stay here?' he said to the woman. 'You've helped me decide something.'

He walked almost past us and disappeared into a large door at the back of the bridge, which seemed to be a storage area.

We heard the scrape of things being moved around, and then a muffled Colin saying, 'Where'd I put it? Nope, that's not it.'

Finally there were a few clanks of metal, and then an animal snort.

The door burst open. Colin trotted out on a horse. He wore a helmet and breastplate. A green belt was buckled around his waist. In one hand he carried a pole with a flying banner attached to it. On the banner was written the words 'The Town and Country Planning Act 1947.'

In the other hand was a lance.

'I am a British Local Government Officer,' he said calmly.

The horse reared, snorted again, and charged.

He caught the Woman directly in the midriff, skewering her like a kebab. He pulled the lance out of her, spurred his horse into full gallop, leapt over piles of junk, and hurled the lance at the Sphinx, even as the Sphinx tried to flap into the sky.

The injured woman, fast transmuting herself back into the Scary Haired Woman with all the arms, scrambled up and followed the Sphinx into the heavens.

Colin drew his sword, spurred his horse again, and leapt into the heavens, towards the fast-scattering cloud of beings.

We could still hear him calling 'I am a British Local Government officer!' as he chased them down with the sword.

We watched him go.

'I think Colin's probably going to be OK,' said Keziah.

'So that's what integrity looks like,' I mused. 'I must try it sometime.'

'How are you with dog poo?' asked Keziah. 'I'll get us some bags.'

# THE HOLY PASSION OF A FRUIT PASTILLE

Lottie would have received my parcel on Saturday morning.

I didn't hear from her that day.

Nor the day after, nor the day after that. Not a text, not a little email, nothing.

*

'Leopold wants a session on my couch. Do come. Clemency.'

A messenger spirit had deposited that note in my soul later that week, which explained how Keziah, Stub and I were now sheltering in the hollow tree in Seasons House, having met up at the *Shepherd Diner* and paused only for a modest midnight lunch of Singaporean chicken rice and plantain fritters.

Through the spyholes we could watch Leopold lying on a leather therapist's couch which Clemency had indulgently supplied. He didn't look well. His face, underneath the fake tan, was yellowish. Welts spotted his skin. The Lady Wisdom, meanwhile, sat quietly at the foot of the couch.

'Have you a cold compress for my forehead?' Leopold was asking. 'I have a thundering headache.'

'Cold compress,' replied Clemency, looking slightly weary despite her impeccable manners. She nodded to one of her interns.

'How does she not strangle him?' asked Keziah.

'She's not you,' I whispered back. This hollow tree forced me to put my face quite close to Keziah's which I didn't like.

'The smells in this place rev up my asthma,' opined Leopold.

'Nothing much we can do about that I'm afraid,' said Clemency. 'Smell of spring.'

'I generally prefer the odours of a night-club,' said Leopold. 'Stale hormones and vomit.'

'Can't help you there,' said Clemency, evenly.

'Well I obviously need to bounce a few ideas around with you,' said Leopold, his hands tucked behind his head, pushing his pony-tail away. 'Between you and me, the war against Mark Bright isn't going quite as well as I'd hoped by this stage.'

'You've tried getting at Mark—'

'My initial investigations confirmed that the previous efforts by my employers were doomed to fail,' snapped Leopold. 'Mark is completely impervious. Blasted integrity. We had hoped for something in his personal financial exposure, perhaps a desire to cut corners … but nothing. He's so relieved to have given up the venture capital world … so much joy, so focussed, it's utterly sick and unnatural. We can't touch him.'

'What about pride?' asked Clemency.

Leopold massaged his forehead.

'Not at the moment. Not even that. Not even the old reliable. It cost him so much to leave his old job and his old girlfriend. He started to doubt himself. Of course it'll come back, we'll get him then, but not at the moment.'

'Hmm,' said the Lady Clemency. 'Bit of a pickle.'

'Then there's Jamie Smith. He's vulnerable enough but he's as bone idle at doing evil as he is at doing good. He's got the holy passion of a fruit pastille.'

'Harsh,' I whispered to Keziah.

'Shush.'

'That leaves Michael Collins.' Leopold was shaking his head. 'He's ripe with potential but hasn't fulfilled it.'

'What about Keziah Mordant?' asked Clemency.

'She's a bit of a handful, to be honest,' said Leopold.

'And anyway,' observed Clemency, 'by focussing on Mark, Keziah, Michael and Jamie you could be accused of hardly bringing anything original to the party.'

'I was coming to that. Obviously we had to try a different approach. Working with Faber and Colin Studd was an original touch,' said Leopold. 'And I thought we had a good plan.'

'Except it failed,' said Clemency. 'Don't you think one mark of a "good plan" is that it succeeds?'

'That idiot Faber lost control of the planning process. That Mordant woman was a complication and it was just bad luck to discover Colin Studd. All these people with integrity on one project? What are the odds? It was a good plan—no, no, put the compress over the eyes, not the forehead, you stupid woman!'

'Leopold,' interrupted Clemency calmly. 'If you speak to my interns like that again I will take the compress, drench it in rocket fuel, insert it somewhere in your person "where the sun don't shine" and apply burning phosphorus. Do you understand?'

'I was merely helping her—'

'Do you understand?'

'I do.'

'You are happy with the compress?'

'Ecstatic.'

'Do carry on. What did your employers think of your plan so far?' asked Clemency.

'They are not in a place to make balanced judgements,' snapped Leopold.

He lapsed into a brooding silence, and Clemency watched him. 'I just *know* I can do something with Julian Faber. He's fuming over having the Oyster Café taken away from him.'

An idea seemed to take hold of Leopold. 'He's not good at his job. His promotion prospects are basically zero. And he's itching to have a cause to fight.'

Leopold sat up on his couch. 'What if I make him sabotage the Oyster Café? Even after it's been taken away from him! *Because* it's been taken away from him! He'd love that!' Leopold swung his feet off the side of the couch.

'But where does that get you?' asked Clemency. 'The plans are going to pass because Colin is going to pass them. It's all going to happen.'

'I don't know,' said Leopold. 'But there's something there. Secrecy, power, self-importance for Julian. He craves respect. And loads of money sloshing around. I need to do some research … and I've got to take charge. This needs my personal touch. I need to be directly in command.'

'That's going to be a hard sell to the Woman, the Dog, the Sphinx and the Bull,' said Clemency. 'They prefer you as consultant.'

'Small minds!' sputtered Leopold. 'It's for the Cause!'

'Not sure they'll understand that.'

'Look. I've got to meet up with them again. I've got to try to persuade them.'

'Meet here,' said Clemency. 'We've got plenty of space. I'll come along.'

'You won't, er, let on that I came here for advice? Obviously part of my marketing appeal is that I am intellectually one step ahead of those who employ me. I must preserve Brand Leopold.'

'Brand Leopold,' said Clemency.

'Yes,' said Leopold.

'Good luck with that,' said Clemency. 'Find a convenient time.'

'Tomorrow's Hallowe'en,' said Leopold. 'They'll all be busy. How about the day after? OK. That's settled.

'And you know, I'm not sure I needed to come here at all. I pretty well figured everything out myself.'

And he flew off.

Keziah and I waited for him to disappear, then unfolded ourselves out of the tree stump.

'That's all good,' I said. 'Leopold's leaving us alone and focussing on Julian Faber.'

I noted that Keziah and Clemency shared a glance.

'Possibly,' said Clemency.

'Well that's what he said,' I said. 'If that's what he said, that's what he said.'

Clemency rubbed the end of her nose with a finger. 'Unless that's what he wanted us to hear.'

'He didn't know we were here. We were hiding.'

'He knows we're targeting him,' said Keziah. 'He might guess that we come down here.'

'Your problem, Keziah, is that you can take the lawyer out of the courtroom but you can't take the courtroom out of the lawyer. You're just making things up.'

'And my problem?' asked The Lady Wisdom, with a raised eyebrow.

'Obviously *you* don't have any problems because you're the Personification of Divine Wisdom,' I stuttered. 'But it's possible you may be over-indulgent to Keziah. Possibly. Rather than stamping out sloppy thinking straight off. Which is kind, I get that. But I mean he said what he said. We heard him.'

'Indeed,' said Clemency.

'He wouldn't stage something like that, just to put us off the scent?'

'Possibly not,' said Clemency.

'I mean this is Leopold we are talking about. Is he that cunning? I doubt it.'

'He is, however,' said Clemency, 'trying to take charge of the operation. That would widen his scope to act.'

'In any case, it's easy to tell. If he attacks Julian Faber I'm obviously right.'

'A reassuring thought,' said Clemency.

# A YEAR'S WORTH OF NICE THINGS

Stub drove us back to the *Diner*.

'You seem quiet,' I said to him. 'You all right?'

We had left Seasons House far behind and Stub had set the pengub on a straight course up to the navigation light of the *Diner*, which glowed like a star, far above us.

'Every so often, sir,' said Stub, 'Darkness masses in my mind.'

This was no surprise. Regular and eternal as the sea, Stub swung from desperation-to-please to morose and sullen terror. In a world of change, the regularity was reassuring.

'Worried about the ending again?'

'Who among the demons would not be, sir?'

'You've never thought, everything might turn out fine in the end?'

'That on the Great Day of Judgement, it'll be alright on the night?'

'Yes.'

'I often think that sir. But I find that is an illusion I cannot sustain.'

'You don't know everything.'

'I know this, sir. The Almighty will cleanse every spot of evil out of his Universe. Like an antibiotic or a sterilizing fluid washing away every spot of dirt.'

'A problem if you happen to think you are a spot of dirt?'

'Or if I am so judged. Indeed sir. Eternally burnt up and consumed by incandescent light.'

'That's the plan?'

'That would seem to be his plan, sir, yes.'

'Ah, there's probably a get-out somewhere. It might not be true, for one thing.'

'Most helpful, sir.'

'What does Jonah advise?'

'I have a great respect for the Old Testament prophet but I am afraid he and I do not see eye to eye on this matter.'

'So what *does* he advise?'

'He advocates total surrender. The Lady Clemency offers a similar perspective, sir.'

'You don't believe them?'

'It is a counsel of despair. It is also too easy. It cannot be so simple. Surely I must find my own way up this great hill. I must attain the quest myself.'

'On a scale of 1-10,' I said, 'approximately how far up the hill are you?'

'I am not even on the hill,' said Stub. 'And I am digging down.'

'Not brilliant then,' I said.

'No sir.'

*

Kirsty had left us some food and drink for our return: Papua New Guinean coffee for me and a hot chocolate for Keziah with cream, marshmallows, and milk, white and dark chocolate sprinkles. Kirsty had filled a plate for me with digestive biscuits and thick slabs of Cheshire cheese, all the better for being enjoyed in the calorie-free heavens. She'd left a small ingot of ultra-dark chocolate for the lawyer.

Stub, who hated food, paced heavily over to some shady corner of the Lido, the better to sit and brood, so it was just Keziah and me.

I munched my digestives and Keziah sipped her chocolate.

'Stub's heading for the emotional exit again,' I said. 'Actually you don't look that bright either.'

Keziah had spent the journey leaning back in the chariot and staring upwards. She looked exhausted, which was not like her. Anger usually kept her energy levels at peak charge. 'Nice thing about this job. The relentless cheerfulness of my colleagues.'

'Whatever,' she said, not even raising a curse.

I sighed. I was aware that the fearsome little firebrand wasn't an over-backed pony in the friendship stakes. And that over the months, we kind of owed each other. Even if she didn't entirely see that. Or perhaps she did. Anyway. Jamie's good deed for the half-year.

'We've been busy,' I said.

'That's not it.'

'This might not be totally my business—'

'Then shut up.'

'OK.'

Keziah glowered at me. 'Sorry,' she said.

'Of course,' I tried again. 'I'm with Mark quite a lot. He doesn't talk about you obviously. But I do get a kind of impression.'

Keziah didn't stop me talking, so I carried on. 'My impression is that he can't—I don't know—get anywhere.'

'He needs to be patient.'

'He needs to be a saint. He spends an evening with you and you spend the whole time acting like you wish he wasn't there.'

'That's what he said?'

'No. That's my impression of his impressions. So it's a second-order derivative of the actual situation. I just wondered if you were being entirely fair to him.'

'Obviously not,' snapped Keziah.

Keziah, I thought in passing, would be a good name for a brand of refrigerator. Always frosty and buckets of ice whenever you need them.

'The thing is, I suspect he might be very fond of you.'

Keziah said nothing but looked very miserable.

'Why else would he keep asking you out?'

'I don't know why.'

'Look I'm a completely disinterested observer, OK? But even I can see he could find you totally adorable. Because you're such an utterly passionate fighter. Even though you spend most of your energy fighting yourself. There's nobody you treat worse than you treat yourself, there's nobody you speak to more harshly than you speak to yourself, and there's nobody you criticize more than yourself. But if someone can get beyond being collateral damage in your personal civil war they can unearth something precious.'

'Thank you.'

'But if you keep treating Mark like something you've found on your shoe, which I don't think is how you feel about him, he'll give up and go away. Not because he isn't fond of you but because he thinks he gets the message.'

'Are you finished?'

'Certainly hope so,' I said. 'I've just used up a year's worth of nice things to say about you.'

Keziah fell silent.

'Well?' I asked.

'Conversation over.'

'Are you scared? We all get scared.'

'Conversation over.'

'I'll ask Stub. Everybody gets scared.' I called across the *Diner*. 'Are you scared Stub?'

'I'm scared of eternal perdition, sir. And so should you be.'

*

Thursday evening I arrived home from my day at Madge's, pushed open the door and found my parcel lying on the floor.

It hadn't been opened. Lottie's own loopy handwriting spelled out the words 'Return to sender.' She had crossed out her address and drawn a little arrow to point back to mine.

Lottie knew it was from me, because of my return address on the address label. She knew it was a carefully selected set of dreamily expensive chocolates, because the company logo was there too. Stem ginger, truffles, and me. What girl could resist?

She knew or guessed all that and she hadn't even opened it.

This was my only link with her since her adventures with Umberto. I traced my finger for a moment over where her biro had scratched. Then I took the chocolates outside and threw them in the bin.

# ALL I ASK IS A CHANCE TO DISPLAY MY BRILLIANCE

Keziah and I were busy the next night too, with our usual work.

We tended Derek O'Malley who was still camping in the car park, in a sort of neon-lit gloom, not picked up by an outreach team, not yet doing anything bad enough to get him back in jail. Despite our sticking plaster, it wasn't going to last.

We visited a host of other souls, most of them depressed or self-harmers, trying to smooth out the entrenched views, push back assumptions, spark new hope.

As usual, we weren't conspicuously successful.

*

We arrived early enough at Seasons House to be safely in our hide before Leopold showed up for his pre-arranged meeting with the Four.

We were obliged to watch him practising his arguments a few times before Clemency appeared and then the Bull, the Dog, the Scary Haired Woman with all the arms and the Sphinx, these middle managers and senior stall-holders who had seized power in Vanity Fair ten earthly months ago. It was going to be a difficult meeting.

'Thank you for coming,' Leopold said, as the four Vanity Fair leaders variously sipped, munched, disdainfully refused, or lapped up the food put out by Clemency's interns. 'I thought this was a good place to come to a wise decision about our next moves.'

'Just so we're all clear,' said the Sphinx, dangerously, 'Mark Bright seems immune. Jamie Smith is widely agreed by either side to be not worth bothering with.'

('Do not jab people in the elbows,' I hissed to Keziah, with dignity.)

'Michael Collins has resisted us, despite his vulnerability. And Keziah Mordant—you seem oddly reluctant to single her out for special treatment.'

'That's complicated. We think on the whole—'

'He's scared of her,' growled the Dog.

'*Everybody's* … I mean the point is,' spluttered Leopold. 'Nobody said this was going to be easy. I personally am not discouraged. I think our action so far may be characterised as a series of tactical feints. Leaving them wide open to our main attack, our great move.'

'I thought the move in the Planning Department was the *great move*,' drawled the Sphinx.

'That was merely the first salvo,' insisted Leopold. 'We are going to exploit Julian Faber again. But this time we are going to get him into political intrigues and money-making that might even be illegal. We're going to give him a taste for power and corruption.'

A silence fell. The Dog lay slumped on the floor, unable, like most dogs, to stand on four legs and think at the same time. The Woman ran several of her hands through the hair. The Bull munched on his hay.

'That's not really our thing,' rasped the Dog thoughtfully. 'I mean, you know where you are with depression.'

'Depression is not going to energise him to work for us,' said Leopold.

'What I think is we need to charge into something, hard, and gore it with our horns, and, and…' said the Bull. "That would sort it out.'

'I sympathize with the need for drastic action,' said Leopold. 'And time is running out. I feel we need to bring in a big gun.'

'What's that then?' asked the Bull, interested.

'I myself,' said Leopold. 'While I have appreciated your leadership, there is a sense in which I have felt myself hampered. I have not had the full scope to operate. I am reluctant to move from the shadows of consultancy and—tentatively—suggest myself in a leadership role. But I must.'

'He wants to take over,' said the Dog.

'I do,' agreed Leopold. 'And it has advantages for you. You will have discharged your duties perfectly— by hiring me. I will take all blame if it fails but naturally we must share the credit when it succeeds.'

'You were in charge before,' said the Dog. 'That didn't end well.'

'It hasn't ended yet,' snapped Leopold.

'Just to be sure,' said the Bull, 'if it all goes wrong who gets the blame?'

'I do,' said Leopold. 'But it won't.'

'Doesn't sound too bad,' admitted the Bull after further thought. 'We never wanted this fight. We just wanted to get on with our jobs.'

'And what do you get out of it?' drawled the Sphinx.

'A chance to display my brilliance. And take meticulous revenge against that Mordant woman.'

'What about you?' The Scary Haired Woman asked Clemency, who until now had not said anything.

'I can see the wisdom in it,' said Clemency.

'Absolutely,' said Leopold. 'It's gold-plated.'

Over the next minutes, grumbling, reluctant and anxious, the meeting broke up.

*

Back in our hollow tree I removed my face from the spy-hole and looked at Keziah. 'Told you,' I said. 'I knew it was Julian.'

# A FIDUCIARY DUTY

So we had to stake out Julian Faber's soul, ready for Leopold's attack. And we discovered the Junior Planner just could not get himself to bed.

Julian's soul was a model of the Westminster parliament complex, where evidently he spent much of his fantasy-time. He had distracted himself from his bedtime routine to enjoy a prolonged role-play about answering questions in parliament at Prime Minister's Question Time.

We sneaked into the chamber as a series of Tory former prime ministers raised issues. Julian answered with a brilliant Marxist analysis, delivered with searing wit. Worse, he kept doing retakes until he got it perfect.

It was a full fifty-five minutes, earth time, when he should have been cleaning his teeth, before he strode out of the House of Commons on his soul. He stepped over Tory Prime Ministers, who were sitting on the floor, shaking their heads and saying to themselves, 'If only I'd seen this! How could I be so stupid?'

Julian left the House of Commons and walked to the model of 10 Downing Street on the edge of his soul, passing easily through adoring, banner-waving crowds, offering a smile of recognition here, a friendly joke there, a handshake and a hug.

'Julian Faber,' one of the placards read, 'Prime Minister for life!'

Keziah and I followed him through to the crowd of sighing female journalists who stood outside No. 10.

'I wanted to hold him to account,' we heard one saying as we squeezed past them. 'But he's just so *cute*.' She had *Daily Hate* on her messenger bag.

'I know,' agreed another, whose badge implied she worked for the *Daily Declaim*, incorporating the *Health-Scare and House Price Alert*, 'That cheeky smile!'

'And so smart!' said a third, from the *Left-of-Centre Bumwad*.

'Oh, he's just gorgeous!' giggled the woman from the *Hate*. 'He's certainly won me over to his side! Of the argument! Or the bed!'

('I would say Julian has one or two problems,' I whispered to Keziah.)


We cautiously followed Julian into 10 Downing Street and into the Cabinet Room, which was evidently the place from which Julian steered his soul. Following him wasn't hard, so long as you hung around with crowds of adoring female journalists.

What was he doing?

What was Leopold going to do him?

Leopold was standing in the Cabinet Room. He was giving a presentation. He was surrounded by the great Labour party leaders and cabinet members of the post-war era.

'So, ladies and gentlemen,' he concluded. 'It doesn't need to be this way. Ah, Prime Minister'—he inclined his head toward Julian—'allow me to summarize your thinking.'

'Oh, right,' said Julian.

Leopold cleared his throat.

'Your comrades think you should act, Prime Minister. I am here to tell you how. Sometimes you have to work for the higher good, Julian, do you agree?'

'Of course I do,' said Julian.

'Can you sit on the sidelines while local council provision is privatised? Sold off to a former Venture Capitalist in unholy league with the Church?'

'Oh, that,' said Julian.

'Yes. That,' rejoined Leopold. 'This is a small battle, but it could define you. It is a step to national prominence. Do you think this Oyster Café is really going to help the needy? Course it's not. The man behind the Café is a *vulture capitalist*. If he isn't exploiting the poor he's dodging taxes and it's just wrong. Big business can get its tentacles into everything, even the most vulnerable in society.'

'Can I just stop you there?' said Julian. 'Colin took that planning application off me. What can I do?'

'And then the Church, what's that doing? Shoring up its waning influence by shabby backroom deals, same old story of power and money and exploitation.'

'Yeah, all fine,' said Julian. 'But I've only been a junior planner for eighteen months and I don't have a lot of say.'

'What are you going to do? Wait for Colin to die? In twenty years? Soft power, Julian. Soft power.'

'What does that exactly mean?' asked Julian.

'It only takes a spark to make a fire,' said Leopold. 'And you have the match. Look, everything about that Oyster Cafe project is in the public domain. Right?'

'Yes.'

'But nobody's done anything about it, correct?'

'Yes.'

'Why? Because it's just being sneaked in, alongside boring extensions and new builds.

'Nobody's standing up with an alternative vision.'

Leopold sighed. 'You have this hub for the homeless, this mega-hub, preying on the vulnerable. A massive centre like some huge hairy wart on the sweet, quirky face of Mill Road.

'You have lines of homeless people waiting outside, drinking, hassling passers-by, throwing up in flowerpots, getting into fights, smashing shop windows probably. What's that going to do for the local area? What's that going to do for the shops? Are women going to be able to walk the streets in peace? This is *feminist issue*, Julian!'

'A feminist issue!' Julian blinked behind his owlish glasses. 'But I don't still see … I can't do anything.'

'You can't do anything as a *planner*,' hissed Leopold. 'You can do everything as a *private citizen*. You can make phone calls. You can pull strings. And it's your duty!

'Look around this table,' went on Leopold. 'Are these popular heroes people who sat back and worried about their careers? Aren't they those who stood up and fought for the working man?'

'And woman,' said Julian.

'And woman,' said Leopold.

'Alright, if I believed you, what could I do?' asked Julian.

'What is the point,' said Leopold, 'of having a friend, an ideological soulmate who is the editor of the *Cambridge Argus and Telegraph?* He fills two whole pages with his column every week. You might help him by quietly pointing out to him things that are in the public domain, that frankly he should have noticed himself but hasn't.'

'Well he's been busy on his Venezuela campaign …'

Leopold proposed a fresh location for Venezuela, not on any map, and frankly unlikely to fit where he suggested.

'This is a local issue Julian! This can fire up local people! Shop workers! Ordinary hardworking people! Making their way in the world! Businesses ruined! What about the ayuverdic vegan restaurant just for one example? On a knife edge. This could push it over!'

'Over a knife edge?'

'You know what I mean! Back comes the regressive, conservative, meat-eating tide. All because you failed to stand up.

'And what are you a member of the Labour Party for?'

'It's the committees mostly,' said Julian. 'I wouldn't know what to do on an evening otherwise.'

'You are in the Labour Party,' insisted Leopold, 'to forge a better world for working people.'

'I still don't get this.'

'Make a fuss, Julian! Not as a planner. As a concerned citizen. Put it out there to your local councillors, who sit on the planning committee, right?'

'Right.'

'Then suggest to Nick at the *Cambridge Argus and Telegram* that he interviews the councillors about the new proposed megahub for the homeless.'

'But what if local people aren't worried?'

'They will get worried when they're told to be worried!' Leopold was getting exasperated. Maybe he had underestimated Julian's stupidity. 'Maybe you can get the Party to organise a campaign. Could be an election issue.'

'What do we think?' Julian looked around at the figments of the imagination on his cabinet table, and it seemed that the socialist worthies of the past years all agreed, which was a bit of a miracle.

'That's just the start,' said Leopold. 'Do you remember that person you met at a party? Developer.'

'The one who said we can't have eyes and ears everywhere?'

'Yes. And who said we never bribe but we do give thankyous to people who point things out for us. Highlight things.'

'I do remember him.'

'I think he mentioned the sum of £5K.'

'I think he did.'

'Five Ks. You could take your girlfriend Agnes on a European Rail Break.'

'Or I could enjoy myself,' muttered Julian.

'Well listen up. You call him. Quietly. Concerned member of the public. Isn't he interested in all those square feet of chapel which could be turned into mixed-use accommodation? Perhaps three storeys. You might even get away with four. Bijou flats—for working people. Ethnic shops. Space for startup companies. Who knows?

'And *then* tell the developer a £5K thank-you present would be nice but £10K would mean that you were even more vigilant and full of helpful suggestions in the future.'

'Yeah, but what could developers do?' asked Julian. 'They don't own the building.'

'They stir up trouble. They talk to the newspapers. They say, "that controversial building on Mill Road— not sold yet—We have alternative plans. They can sigh wistfully. If only we had the building. They can even submit alternative plans—you don't need to have a stake in a building to submit plans for it. You could even *help* them submit alternative plans.'

'This I know,' said Julian.

'For a fee,' said Leopold. 'So. Public opinion is swayed, which sways the Planning Committee, who overrule the evil Colin. They turn down the plans. You defeat everybody, you win a victory for the people, and you get ten grand in your pocket. And a lot of respect.'

'OK, but what if the Planning Committee don't turn down the original plans?'

'You can still win the day.'

'How?'

'Oh Julian. Point out that these Swivel-Eyed and Fragmented Baptists, or whatever they are called, have a fiduciary duty to sell their charitable assets to the highest bidder. Which will be your developers.'

'A what?'

'Fiduciary.'

'Can I write that down somewhere?'

'It will be supplied when you need it,' snapped Leopold. 'All you've got to do is keep your nerve.'

'Is it true?' asked Julian. 'That they have a thingy duty to sell to the highest bidder?'

'It doesn't matter whether it's true or not. What matters is whether the chapel trustees want a long court battle.'

Julian paused while he thought about this. 'What you're suggesting is not actually illegal.'

'No. And don't forget the £10K. £10Ks just waiting for a sharp mind with an eye for an opportunity. Oh, and a passion for working people. Somebody must patrol the walls while the city sleeps, vigilant for capitalist threats. You are that man.'

'Person,' said Julian.

'You are that person,' corrected Leopold.

'It's amazing,' said Julian, 'How I have my best ideas while I'm on the loo.'

'Very fertile mind,' replied Leopold, through his teeth. 'Hardly surprising what comes out.'

'Don't think my life was improved by knowing that,' I whispered to Keziah.

# A KIND OF POSY

'What are we going to do?' I asked Corrie Bright and Jonah, later that same night, back at the *Diner*.

'Break the problem into small pieces,' suggested Corrie. 'Julian is trying to influence councillors against the Oyster Cafe. Well, Michael and Mark can lobby councillors too. Julian is going to organise a press campaign. Mark and Michael can do the same. If the *Argus and Telegraph* won't listen they can go to the local TV and radio, or even to the national papers.'

'But what about a developer putting in a better offer that the Church is legally bound to accept?'

'I don't think that's true,' said Keziah, 'but I think it's true enough to tempt the developers to bring it to court.'

'Which is a problem.'

'Yes.'

'And we're going to—?'

'We'll have to think of something.'

*

The next working day, which was a Monday, was quiet in our stone-lined office at Madge's because Mark was out at meetings and it was Michael's day off. I was fine with this but the coffee machine was snorting and gurgling, issuing steam and rather too much foam, evidently feeling the heat and pressure.

*

I left Madge's in the early evening, and visited a flower stall in the city square.

Cambridge market was atmospheric with its lights bright against the early dusk and the autumn evening depositing an early dew on the striped fabric roofs: bread stalls with flour-dusted bloomers; the cheese shop, tangy and musky; the flower shop itself, staffed with a girl who wore her hair up but let a few brown wisps fall against her cheeks and who wore fingerless gloves and whose breath showed against the bare lightbulbs.

Amazingly you could mail bouquets to anywhere in the world from her outpost of planks and canvas. 'What I'd like,' I said, 'short stems, loads of tiny flowers, a kind of posy, that would look just perfect on a wooden chest of drawers in a cramped bedroom. In Lincolnshire.'

We spent a few pleasant minutes umming and aahing. I wrote a label (same as before) and arranged for it to be sent to Lottie.

Flowers heal, I hoped.

I wasn't giving up.

# NOT TOO SHABBY

On Tuesday Mark phoned Colin Studd to inquire about the planning application.

'Good news and bad news,' Mark said after he clicked off his phone. 'The good news? They are still on track for the plans to go to the planning committee a week on Friday. And this planner sounds a lot more positive than the other one.

'The bad news is that someone else is looking at the property. Some out-of-town developer has put in a speculative request for outline permission to convert the chapel into apartments and shops.'

'Can they do that?' I asked.

'Apparently so.'

'How did they hear?'

'It's all public domain. People look out for these things.'

'But the chapel trustees are still selling to us?'

'In theory. The developers might offer a lot more than we're offering. And in the worst case it's not impossible that the trustees may be obliged to sell to the highest bidder. Part of their duty as trustees.'

'I thought all that had been sorted out already?'

'We think we would win any court case. Our problem is the cost of fighting it. These new developers probably want to make the process so uncomfortable that it just becomes easier to let them have the property.'

'Doesn't sound good.'

'They have weak spots too.'

'I had an idea, by the way. Might help.'

'An idea?'

'Yes.'

'You?'

'Yes.'

'That's the second one.'

'I was thinking—' I pressed on with some dignity—'that all our publicity so far has been written for your millionaire friends and their boards. Fair enough if we're fundraising, which we were.

'Shouldn't we also write some popular stuff, like for the newspapers? I could do some stories about people who've already been helped through Michael.'

'I think we could rustle up some candidates,' added Michael thoughtfully from behind his computer.

'Have you got time?' asked Mark.

'Probably,' I said. 'I'd suggest a press-release type news piece and a feature article or two. All ready in case we needed them.'

'Good,' said Mark.

*

Which all led to a little burst of activity for Jamie. I called the *Argus and Telegraph* and pitched the idea. They weren't enthusiastic but promised to look at it. Through the next days I met and interviewed a couple of former clients of Michael's.

I also interviewed Michael, who quickly got onto the subject of Derek O'Malley. There are people, Michael told me, who have really fallen through the gaps. But they still turn up for lunch at his little twice-weekly Oyster Café at Madge's.

154

If we had more resources and a permanent site, Michael told me, we could do more than give them lunch. We could guide them into all the network of facilities Cambridge offers. No forms to fill in—just people ready to help. And we could rehabilitate them rather than just feed them.

Then Michael told me how the Strict and Particular Baptist chapel could be cheaply converted into a café and homeless hub. It could become a model for provision throughout the country.

He had longed to see this for many years and now all the parts were fitting together.

So after some inspired typing, I had a long feature piece about Michael, with two case-studies as side-bars. I did a press release too, took some photographs, and got the feature piece to the editor Nick at the *Argus and Telegraph*.

He was not nearly as enthusiastic as an editor should have been on receiving well-written stories of local interest, opening the lid on the small-scale heroism in our community.

I presumed Julian Faber had already nobbled him. And even though he wasn't enthusiastic initially, I guessed that despair over the lack of good copy would outweigh all else by Thursday lunchtime, his press deadline.

Though the stories were about the former homeless, I realised that quietly underneath them all was Michael's own story. He had run the small-scale Oyster cafe with volunteers twice a week for years at Madge's.

It was a simple formula but it worked for his chaotic customers. They would come in for the food and might end up getting free chiropody or health advice. They might reconnect with the job centre or the accommodation people. Michael's own willingness to listen to tales of woe, make phone calls, fill forms, write testimonials, oil the wheels with friendly employers, and take phone calls at all hours was obviously key to the whole thing.

It could be so much more if it was permanent and well-staffed, rather than temporary and ad hoc.

It also turned out Michael, who was not a wealthy man, paid court fines for his clients, came with them to the police station and visited them in hospital. This disorganized, vaguely academic cleric had been quietly responsible for turning around many lives.

I supposed only Keziah, Corrie, Jonah and I knew about his lonely battles with his mind, and the way those battles spiralled into a desire for underage flesh. I was glad that he had never actually indulged his taste.

*

Doing these pieces gave me a surprising, happy buzz.

And how many lives have *I* changed, I wondered idly after shipping the copy to the *Argus and Telegraph*.

No need for false modesty here. I did order a taxi, at least twice a month, to pick up Lizzie from whatever doorstep she was crying on at three in the morning after closing time at *Vodka Vodka Vodka*.

And there were my annual heroics for Kidney Research, dividing my loose change into twelve different envelopes—so pretending I'd done a street collection for them—and sending them back.

Not to mention working with Keziah on saving the Universe.

All that should be worth something.

Shouldn't it?

# THE SWELLING GROUNDSWELL

Nothing from Lottie after my nice gift of flowers. She was probably holding back so as not to seem over-keen.

Hard to think of any other reason.

*

On the Thursday morning the office received an unexpected phone call from the *Argus and Telegraph* asking for a phone conference with Mark and Michael.

Were they aware of the groundswell—the swelling groundswell—against their proposed gigantic homeless megahub on the fragile cityscape of Mill Road?

How did they think the Planning Committee could possibly approve it?

Was it true that Mark was using the whole scheme to avoid taxes?

What other explanation was there for his swift departure from the celebrated local venture capitalists Wood, Main and Bright?

Mark and Michael, somewhat wearily, answered these questions as best they could, before Nick rang off, citing his deadline.

'I'm glad you sent those stories to the *Argus and Telegraoh.*' Michael had said after coming off the phone. 'But I'm not sure they had the desired effect.'

'Hardly Jamie's fault,' said Mark.

'The swelling groundswell,' mused Michael.

'And there isn't one,' said Mark. 'Or wasn't until he tried to create one. But why would he do that?'

'He likes something to rant about in his column,' I said.

'A pain, though,' said Mark.

'Cappuccino?' I asked. 'The coffee machine's gagging to help.'

'Thank you,' said Mark. 'Even though it's only the weekly free rag, we need to do something.'

'Don't counter them directly,' I suggested. 'Just put some more good-news stories elsewhere. I think some of these people I interviewed wouldn't mind being on the local telly.'

'OK,' said Mark. 'And we should probably call up some councillors ourselves. Michael? Looks like we need to switch into schmooze-mode.'

'Schmoozing now,' said Michael.

*

Mark started working the phones, and I began to glimpse why he impressed people. He had evidently put together a contact list on the fly, in his head, and started leafing through it, calling local media, local politicians, and rich and influential friends. He was patient and charming, informal and self-deprecating.

By mid-afternoon he had guaranteed that local TV would be running stories about the quiet movement to rehabilitate street people in Cambridge, and how the work was going to expand into a permanent site on the hospitable and welcoming Mill Road.

Councillors on the Planning Committee had received phone calls from him and (though they didn't know it yet) were also going to receive calls in the coming days from politicians, well-known Cambridge business leaders, academics, criminologists, the odd local celebrity and a former Archbishop of Canterbury.

Michael was going to be busy showing media teams around and arranging media opportunities for some of his clients. I was going to generate more copy for journos.

A dusting of positive publicity.

*

On Friday the weekly *Argus and Telegraph* came out. In his two-page column the editor tried to throw mud at the Oyster Cafe project. But he had been unable to put together any suspicious connections or unearth a groundswell of opposition. He only had one actual quote from a rent-a-rant councillor friend of his whom he always approached when capitalism needed a good kicking.

Lacking facts, he could only raise a lot of questions and ended his column with a defiant, 'clearly this ill-conceived project should be put firmly on ice until these serious issues are addressed, perhaps through a full Public Inquiry.'

He had compressed my good-news story into two paragraphs elsewhere in the paper and deleted any reference to Michael or the Oyster Cafe.

Yet by early the next week it was clear we were going to win this battle.

A light spray of media stories briefly caught the air: innovation was coming to the some of the most intractable social problems of our city, powered by unsung local heroes and entrepreneurial philanthropy. An enlightened local council and hospitable local people were supportive. Beyond old political distinctions of left and right, the solutions combined social justice, volunteerism, corporate social responsibility and responsive public services.

Better still, the stories were even true.

*

Tuesday at Madge's saw us fielding a few more media queries while Mark tried to make sure everything was in place for the planning committee decision on Friday. He kept in touch with Elspeth, Chair of the Trustees of the three-strong congregation at the Strict and Particular Baptist Chapel. The other two members of the congregation were the other two Trustees.

Elspeth, Mark assured us, was still keen to sell the Chapel to us, and hadn't received any other offers.

So all we needed was:

Planning permission granted on Friday

No other offers, and no threat of a legal challenge.

We were going to win.

A bit of heavenly work, a bit of earthly work, Leopold was going to be defeated and the Oyster Café was going to happen.

And none of us was going to the Sump of Lost Dreams.

# A LETTER FROM LOTTIE

I pushed open my door on Tuesday evening and felt it clearing a path through the paper that had been stuffed into my letterbox.

Among the pizza fliers and the people offering to pay cash for my gold earrings was a letter in Lottie's friendly, rounded hand. I heard blood rushing in my ears as my heart pumped.

In these days when you can squirt a packet of electrons from Lincolnshire to Cambridgeshire by a dozen different means, she had chosen the old-fashioned way.

Typical Lottie, choosing the literary and intimate. For a special message. And not difficult to imagine her gazing out of her Lincolnshire garret, seagulls gliding over the potato fields, and writing something like this:

*Dear Jamie,*
*I've come to my senses.*
*It's been tough recently but I see it all now.*
*I'm so sorry I've been pushing you away. You've changed — I see that now. I've changed too. I see that now as well.*
*Perhaps you're right. Perhaps it's time for us to start writing a fresh page together. Will it be a short story or a lifetime's adventure?*
*It'll be fun to found out.*
*Call me.*

*Love Lottie.*

I dropped the pizza fliers and the gold leaflet into the recycle basket and walked over to my sofa, heart pounding even faster.

I swan-dived backwards on the sofa, plumped the cushion under my head, took a breath, and opened the letter.

I unfolded its three folds.

*Dear Jamie*
*Please stop harassing me.*
*Lottie.*

I stared at it.

Look, I only recently got out of a coma and my emotions may still be a little bit shot.

My eyes started filling up.

*

I still had not drawn the curtains, despite it being dark outside and the central heating being on, when my sister Lizzie—with whom I shared the house— came home.

She saw the letter and gave me a hug and wanted to talk about it. I did not want to talk about it. What was there to talk about? I was fired. Talk about it? What a good idea. Let's go over it all again and make it hurt more.

No thank you.

Would I like a drink, then?

I've got some tea.

I meant something stronger.

No. Pouring transport fuel down your neck gives you cancer and fat legs.

Does it really give you fat legs?

It was a metaphor for general dissolution you airhead.

General who?

Never mind.

*

Before going to bed, I texted Keziah.

*I know we were supposed to get together at 2:00am. Sorry I can't make it.* Then I pondered for a few moments, pondered again, and added, *Lottie sacked me.*

When my phone did its *mmmph mmmph mmmph* vibrating thing at exactly 2:00am, I snatched it up, jabbed the button and snapped at Keziah:

'Who died?'

'Good morning.'

'Didn't you get my text?'

'Jamie you can't just dip out.'

'I specifically—'

'There is too much going on. By the way, I told Corrie and Jonah about Lottie.'

'Oh thank you very much. Wonderful. No doubt Kirsty's broadcasting it the length and breadth of the Omniverse. I expect everyone's having a good laugh. I expect Kirsty's organising an "I-told-you-so" party where everyone can come and point their fingers—'

Keziah suggested I shut up.

I shut up.

'Do you know where your soul is?'

'No,' I said. 'Yes.'

'You're in the Sump. You're in the *Sump*, Jamie.'

'Good.'

'Listen. Corrie and Jonah have fixed something up. Do you want to go and see Lottie's soul?'

'When?'

'Now.'

'I thought she wasn't in our area.'

'They made some calls. Lincolnshire has a Sump too.'

'Lottie's in the Sump of Lost Dreams?'

'Let's see. Domestic abuse. Divorce. Shame. Going home to mum. And she lost a baby.'

'She lost a baby?'

'Kirsty told me. In Mexico. Tends to happen when someone stamps on your womb.'

'She didn't tell me that.'

'In my experience, it's not the sort of thing you bring up in conversation,' said Keziah. 'But it's normal in domestic abuse. She gets pregnant, he gets violent.'

Even in my dulled emotions I found room to make a note somewhere that if I was ever having a chat with Keziah and it started veering towards to the subject of fetuses-I-have-lost-in-my-wild-past, to steer the talk to football or something. 'Yes, she's in the Sump, Jamie. Very deep. And she doesn't think she'll ever get out.'

'So we're both in the Sump.'

'Yes.'

'What do you think that means?'

'Leopold was fooling us.'

'*What?* You think he was behind this?'

'Perfect for him Jamie. Sadness, anger, bitterness. So much for him to play with.'

'But those conversations with Clemency ...'

'He was playing us, Jamie. He figured we were listening in.'

'All that stuff about Julian?'

'A distraction.'

'And all the time Leopold was messing with Lottie?'

'Lottie's husband messed with Lottie. He only had to stir you up. Tug at a few longings. You would do the rest.'

Keziah let this sink in.

'Even if that's true,' I said. 'Why would he attack me? Even I don't think I'm all that indispensable.'

'We thought about that.'

'Oh.'

'You might be a distraction. While we're trying to fix you he attacks someone else.'

'Charming. Wonderful. And your cunning response is?'

'To fix you.'

# THE SUMP OF LOST DREAMS

What, and where, is the Sump of Lost Dreams? My soul had found it easily enough, of course, crashing through the heavens after reading Lottie's letter, but it isn't so easy to picture it.

For us space-dependent mortals, it helps to picture the Golden Censer near the top and Pandemonium at the bottom. Earth itself is far below that. (Above the Censer is a Surface, beyond which it is possible to hear a party.)

Perhaps it's easiest for us spatial-types to think of the heavens as a series of layers, and the Sump as a kind of drainage layer snaking through the heavenly places like a cold current of slime.

Jonah and Corrie joined Keziah on my soul, which was good if you wanted to navigate quickly to the Lincolnshire Sump. But not so fine if you wanted, as I wanted, to conceal my soul's wretched state from as many eyes as possible.

*

'Kirsty sent some tiffins,' said Corrie, handing over a pile of three scalding hot tins held together by a leather strap.

The four of us were standing on what was left of Lottie-land on my soul, and they were polite enough to ignore the devastation all around us.

I set the tins down and opened them.

'Indian finger food,' I said. 'Anyone like some?' The women declined but I managed to press a samosa on the Prophet Jonah, who, like me, believes in eating regardless of the current crisis.

'How did I get here?' I asked.

'Leopold just had to intensify what you were already feeling,' said Corrie. 'Maybe block up your ears so you didn't listen to advice. And he distracted you with Julian and plenty of work.'

Lottie-land all around us was trashed. I had gently steered my memories of Lottie into a large house on my soul where I hoped they would be happy without me ever meeting them again. (Though I doubted it. Multiple Lotties were likely to have a brittle relationship without a Jamie around to loosen them up.)

That left all my hopes, dreams, ambitions and, yes, one or two fantasies about Lottie and these I had doused with fuel and set alight. Black smoke from them billowed into the heavens.

All this I had done while laying on my sofa after receiving Lottie's note.

And while falling into the Sump of Lost Dreams.

'The Sump of Lost Dreams is not the sort of place you want to leave your soul for any length of time,' said Jonah.

He was right. The air and sky around us was brownish, chilling, toxic.

An awkward silence fell.

'You do want to get out, Jamie,' said Corrie. This was halfway between an inquiry and an instruction.

'I didn't choose to fall into the Sump,' I said. 'Anyone for a mini-bhaji?'

I handed one to Jonah but I was aware that no-one was saying anything. 'I get it. I didn't choose to come here but I can choose whether I stay.'

'For the moment you can,' said Corrie.

'I don't know where else I can go,' I said. 'You can see how much of my soul Lottie took up. I've loved Lottie since she first started pointing out my faults.'

'The reason we're going to see her soul,' said Corrie more gently than her Scottish abruptness usually let her be, 'is to see how things are with her. And to try to heal you.'

'Have you been in touch with Lincolnshire Soul Team? Is there such a thing?'

'There is and we have,' said Corrie.

'Why haven't they done something about Lottie then?'

'They have, and they continue.'

'Well they're not doing a very good job.'

'Here's how we get to see Lottie,' said Jonah. 'Bit of spatial movement, bit of intuition and imagination, all precisely calibrated. Fortunately not difficult. Er— and we need to hold hands.'

I am not a massive fan of handholding but I found myself reaching for Keziah's limp little hand on one side and Jonah's surprisingly rough paw on the other. Keziah was equally reluctant and we brushed fingers as little as possible.

'OK,' said Jonah. 'Here we go.'

With a rush of thought such as happens when you have a sudden flash of insight, we landed in an instant on Lottie's soul. Or rather, on a thick layer of ice covering it.

Around us was the darkness, gloom and dripping acid of the Sump of Lost Dreams, that corrosiveness that (now I think about it) strips all the softness from souls, making them jagged and unyielding, and that cracks them deep inside, so that they both live in pain and deal in it. Not a place to go, or stay, yet many people spend large parts of their lives there. The Lincolnshire Sump tasted much the same as Cambridge's.

It was snowing on Lottie's soul, and wind was blowing.

'Don't eat the snow,' said Jonah. 'It's acid. Let's try that hill over there.'

We followed Jonah in a line across the ice, up a small rise.

'Here we are,' said Jonah. Getting to the top of the ridge, we saw a downward slope and a further ridge. A cave opened in the side of the further ridge. 'I think here,' said Jonah, 'is where the Sump above us is thinnest. Keep your eyes on the sky. The Lincolnshire people told us that impact events were common. We should see one if we wait long enough.'

'What kind of impact events?' I asked.

'Meteorites,' said Jonah.

'I can't see anything but the snow,' I said.

We waited.

'There!' pointed Keziah. High above us, a bright star was falling through the snowflakes. It dimmed as it headed towards us, passed over our heads, and landed in the bowl with a hiss of steam. Fizzing, it rested on the ice briefly before melting a little patch of ice and sinking. The meltwater trickled towards the cave entrance.

'Let's wait for the next one,' said Jonah.

'It doesn't seem to have done much,' I said.

We waited, and presently another meteorite fell, crashed, melted.

'About once every minute,' said Jonah. 'Right.' We scrambled down the slope—Corrie, striking out with her walking stick and declining my offer of help—and stepped into the cave. It sloped and spiralled downwards and we only kept from falling by pressing against the cave walls.

'I'm going to create one of those burning torches that they have in the movies,' I said. 'I've always wanted to do that. I never worked out how they didn't go out.' I duly did, but then Keziah said, 'One moment,' and with a flash of thought created an LED lighting system in the ceiling.

'Show off,' I said.

The cave spiralled down and we gingerly stepped through it. Keziah extended the lights as we went, though I kept hold of my torch. I had read fantasy novels and played any number of computer games so I was expecting a monster to step up at any moment, obliging me to deploy the torch in heroic combat duties. For which a row of LEDs would hardly substitute.

Sometimes we found stairs. Occasionally we had to step over the small stream that trickled over the cave floor. No monsters emerged. We must have been walking, stumbling and sliding for a quarter of an hour, going ever deeper, until the cave finally opened out dramatically in front of us.

# YOU CAN ASK THE SAME QUESTION ABOUT SUNSHINE

We all stood still in the cold and gloom.

'Tell me what you can see,' asked Jonah.

'Well I can hardly see anything apart from my torch,' I said. 'It reminds me of being stuck with Lottie in a deep cave in Derbyshire—no, never mind about that.'

'Can you light it up?'

'I'm going to shoot a flare,' I said. 'That's another thing I've always wanted to do.'

With a bit of mental juggling, I created a handheld flare gun.

'Mind where you're pointing that,' said Keziah.

'I'm pointing it at the sky,' I said with dignity.

I squeezed the trigger and the flare arced into the dark void. '3-2-1-*bam*!' I said and on cue, the flare exploded.

'Talk to me,' said Jonah.

I looked around.

'We're standing on Lottie's soul … and under the ice-shell here it's beautifully preserved. All things considered. As you can see it takes the form of a lovely Georgian mansion and grounds. She did have a Mexican-themed extension but obviously that's gone. As for the rest … well it's a bit scuffed. Garden's a bit overgrown. But it's in decent shape. It's all just buried in an ice-cave.'

'What do you think the ice is?' asked Corrie as the flare faded.

'Self-defence mechanism?'

'Good.'

'But she's still in the Sump.'

'And she doesn't see a way out. And why is that a particular problem?'

We thought for a moment.

'This whole ice-cave is a mental construct. Of Lottie's,' Keziah said. 'So if she doesn't believe there's a way out, then there isn't a way out, because she's built it believing it. Her faith in her hopelessness keeps her hopeless.'

'Precisely,' said Corrie. 'How can you escape a prison when your own mind made it?'

'You can't,' I said. 'The only tools you have to dismantle the prison are the same things you made the prison out of. You can't fix yourself without first fixing yourself.

The darkness resumed.

'So why have you brought me here?' I asked. 'I can't see what we can do.'

'The meteorites,' said Keziah.

'Exactly right,' agreed Corrie. 'The Lincolnshire team told us they come direct from the Censer. They are a lot brighter when they set out, and they get dimmed by their passage in the Sump. But they still have heat left and they're melting the ice.'

'Not exactly quickly,' I said.

'No,' agreed Corrie. 'But they'll still work. However sad she is today, on earth the sun will keep rising, birds will keep singing, she will pass babies in the street and they will smile and kick their feet. Drop by drop.'

'And underneath she's still OK.'

'She's fine.'

'It'll take forever,' I said.

'The Greeks had a word that is often translated "forever",' said Jonah. 'But they didn't quite mean what you mean. You don't have an English equivalent. They meant "beyond time's horizon". Or "further than I can see." Which is interesting.'

I knew where this was going.

'Lottie's going to be fine,' I said. 'But as far as I'm concerned, it'll take forever.'

In the flickering light of my torch I noticed that Jonah was eyeing the sky and Corrie was frowning at her fingernails. Only Keziah was looking at me and she had a pained expression that might have been sympathy, or possibly hate, or possibly trapped wind. I was glad because my eyes were stinging again. 'And getting hold of that is my own way out of the Sump.'

Jonah scratched his ear while Corrie scrutinised her fingernails.

'There's really nothing we can do? We can't fit big heaters and start melting the ice or something?'

'They'll just ice her up more,' replied Corrie. 'She'll be OK.'

'Those meteorites,' I asked. 'Why do they come?'

'You could ask the same question about sunshine,' said Corrie.

'Kirsty said the tiffins were just an aperitif,' put in Jonah. 'She was cooking up the main meal at the *Shepherd Diner*. I don't know if we were all ready to get back?'

*

Back at the *Diner*, Corrie busied herself with something and Jonah excused himself as he had duties at the University of Metanarratives. While we waited for the murtabaks to finish baking in Kirsty's clay oven, I said to Keziah, 'Corrie and Jonah are telling me to move on, aren't they? Lottie will recover in her own time.'

'Especially if you don't stand waiting by her side like a puppy that hasn't been fed. Yes.'

'I'd always hoped somehow …'

'She was with somebody else and living in Mexico.'

'Yes. Perhaps I hadn't totally factored that in.'

'Really.'

I thought some more. 'Do you know what Churchill said about American foreign policy? He said that you can always rely on the Americans to do the right thing … after they have exhausted all the alternatives. I might be a bit like that with Lottie. I should've given up hoping long ago.'

I sighed. 'What about you? Do you hope? About Mark?'

'I don't want you talking about that.'

'Keziah. There's only us here. But I don't think your non-obsession with Mark is helping you any more than my obsession with Lottie was helping me.'

'It's fine.' On this point, Keziah was perhaps a bit too sure-sounding.

'That's convincing. You don't think,' I went on, 'your issues with Mark might give an opening to Leopold?'

'They might,' said Keziah. 'If I *had* issues with Mark.'

'Which is why you're keeping your relationship in a pot,' I said, suddenly understanding. 'So that you *don't* have issues with Mark.'

I took Keziah's contemptuous silence as agreement.

'But you moved his pot right into the middle of your soul.'

'It's still in a pot. And I'm keeping it there until … there's no hurry.'

'Until when?'

'Just until.'

'Fine.'

'Except—' I said.

'Except what?'

'Except you look exhausted.'

'I'm fine.'

'Not your usual short-tempered self. Which I kind of miss.'

'Jamie,' said Keziah, 'Do you find lots of people come to you for advice?'

'Er—no, not really.'

'Ever wondered why?'

# A LOOK OF CONCENTRATION AND SURPRISE

I spent Wednesday at work at Madge's in a bit of a daze, a post-Lottie fug. This did not seem to matter much. All the publicity, journalism and copywriting was done.

Wednesday night I went to bed early and sought out my soul. One advantage of my near-death experience was I could speed up things that would normally take months of processing the ordinary way.

Emerging in my captain's chair, I left the cricket pavilion, walked across the pitch and climbed through the hills to that large part of my soul-landscape that I had designated as Lottie-land.

I reached the wall and magicked up a giant eraser, capable of flying autonomously, and steered it along the whole length of the wall, rubbing it out.

My former Lottie-land was quiet. The fires had mostly reduced my hopes of our future into sullen piles of glowing ash. The house into which I had ushered all my true memories of Lottie was still intact and the lights were on.

Probably the Lotties within were diligently re-sorting all the books in the house, stopping to eat packed lunches made frugally of the previous night's left-overs, trying cardigans on, or walking in the gardens, mentally cataloguing the trees and flowers.

With a flick of thought, I created giant heaps of topsoil, dotted all over Lottie-land—thick, black wormy loam. Then I created myself a bulldozer, and started pushing the heaps around.

This was quite a lot of fun. It took several hours to get the landscape how I wanted it, a bit like building a golf-course. I built hills around the house so it was out of immediate sight but at peace with its surroundings, and in a cosy hollow.

I exchanged my bulldozer for a tractor and spent another couple of hours turning over all the soil, ready for new planting. Finally I added some tree saplings to stop the soil eroding from my newly-built hills. I hoped in time they would develop into nice mixed woodland, fluttering and squawking with life. And I left large tracts open, good soil, ready for new memories and hopes to establish themselves.

It was a solid piece of work. I felt so good about myself that I walked back to my cricket pavilion, took my seat, pulled back on the ship's wheel and steered my soul without trouble straight out of the dank and acid of the Sump of Lost Dreams all the way through the heavenly places to the *Shepherd Diner*.

*

Corrie Bright walked over.

'That was good work, Jamie,' she said. She had evidently been waiting for me.

'Not that difficult,' I said. 'I just had to let go my dreams and accept a life of monotone dullness stretching all the way until I fall off my perch.'

'It just might possibly turn out better than that,' said Corrie Bright. 'You never know.'

I grunted.

'I can see you thinking, Jamie,' Corrie continued, as she sat down at my table. 'It's like watching a baby fill its nappy. The look of concentration and surprise.'

'Thanks,' I said.

Kirsty brought her a milk stout on a tray and left.

'For what it's worth,' I said, 'I was thinking that everyone's standing around all the time waiting for me emotionally to catch up.'

'Not necessarily. Have you thought you might be as emotionally well-rounded as any of us?'

I had not thought of this. If I did: Keziah, as well-rounded as a shard of glass, was out of the running and Corrie herself … now I thought about it, brusqueness and brevity were her stock responses to nearly everything, a bit like a cricketer who had learned she could score highly if she restricted herself to just a few shots. What dreams had she let go? What notes on her keyboard were forever unplayed?

'It might be said to be a fairly low bar.'

'Nevertheless you slipped out of the Sump of Lost Dreams. It had no hold on you. A year ago you couldn't have done that.'

Jonah put his head around the entrance to the *Lido*.

'Ready?' he asked.

'Just about. Is Keziah here?'

'Just arrived,' said Jonah.

'I haven't told Jamie yet.'

'Told me what?'

'Do you remember Keziah saying Michael was like a reformed heroin addict?'

'I do. Stable, but she thought vulnerable to a sudden relapse.'

'And you know that we thought Leopold was playing us? Distracting us with Julian Faber? And then distracting us with you? While all the time planning a series of attacks on Keziah and Michael?'

'I remember that's what Keziah thought.'

'Well. The gossip networks have been humming since earlier tonight.'

'And?'

'Michael got a knock on his door. It was a sixteen-year-old girl who was thrown out of her house some months ago. She is extremely vulnerable and desperate for love. She needs a dad but the only intimacy she has ever known is sexual. She has nowhere else to go. She was knocking on Michael's door and he has taken her in. It is past midnight and of course he lives on his own.'

I took all this in. 'The reformed heroin addict has just been offered a syringe.'

'Yes.'

'By Leopold?'

'Probably.'

'Surely he's got enough common sense.'

'You would hope so.'

'But with Leopold pulling on his desires. Stirring his loneliness. Dumping depression and confusion on him?'

'Yes.'

# DEATH IN THE CATHEDRAL

Kirsty had brought two chariots onto the pavement.

Corrie Bright and Jonah took a relaxed view of delegation which usually involved sending Keziah and me to fight near-impossible odds on our ownsies.

Not this time.

'You're coming too?' I asked the Prophet Jonah.

'Yes,' said Jonah, 'Mainly because we think you'd be totally overwhelmed and defeated by the forces massing against us.'

*

Corrie Bright snapped the pengub reins and streaked to Michael's soul.

Keziah followed in our chariot. I clung onto the side.

Nearing Michael's soul, we flew over a few small villages before landing bumpily on the grass. In front was the well-lit cathedral and around us was the quadrangle of old but busy buildings. Michael, Rural Dean, had a rustic soul.

We clambered out of our two chariots, but left the pengubim hitched to them, in case we needed a quick getaway. The two heavenly animals drew up close to each other and began exchanging thought-bubbles.

'So he's going to bed, we think. This girl is in the room next to him,' said Corrie Bright.

'Integrity would be good at this point,' I said.

'There's Michael,' said Keziah, pointing.

The cleric's spirit stood across the close from us, at the head of a small group of people. As we watched, he escorted three of them into one of the buildings, then came back for the rest. The second group he similarly escorted to another building.

'When Michael goes to sleep,' explained Corrie, he's one of these people who likes to review his day and put everything away tidily.'

'He doesn't seem to be bothered by the girl,' I said.

'Not yet,' said Corrie.

Next, we watched as Michael's spirit made its way into the cathedral. We heard a snatch of choral singing and glimpsed candles as he pushed open the cathedral door, walked in, then closed the oak behind him.

'He has a devotional life,' said Corrie.

'Part of his job, I suppose,' I replied. 'Keep with the edgy frontier of choral plainsong.'

'The danger is when he's done everything and turned out the light,' said Jonah.

While Michael worshipped, we walked down the gently sloping track towards a river. Here Michael grew his soulish flowers and vegetables. Here also, in the soft earth of his soul, he had dug tunnels and stocked them with illicit fantasies and lurid images.

Back in the spring, five months ago, he had almost lost everything when he all-but made a phone call and started living out his fantasies for real. I'd stopped him, driving to his house on earth while Keziah and Corrie fought a desperate battle on his soul.

Since then, he'd partnered with Mark. He had blocked up the tunnels and surrounded them with warning signs to himself. Keziah and I had helped him. He had not, so far as we knew, visited them again.

Jonah, Corrie, Keziah and I sheltered behind a stack of dead wood that Michael had collected to burn.

Presently Michael appeared, now in gardening clothes, took a hoe from his garden shed and started disturbing some weeds.

Corrie and Jonah kept scanning the sky, though to me the heavens looked clear of soul-sucking Vanity Fair machinery, or invading hordes of evil beings.

'There,' said Keziah.

A young girl was walking towards Michael. Her clothes were a tangle, too adult. She had a lovely figure and a teeth-brace and her teeth were black. She looked at Michael, half-aggressive, half-vulnerable.

Michael stood in a daze, blinking.

'Hello,' he said.

'Hello,' she smiled, and gently squeezed his hand.

The touch seemed to electrify him.

He looked at her.

'I'm only entertaining a thought,' he said.

The girl shrugged. 'No harm in that.'

'We can have some tea. Just pop into this tunnel here. We can just dig through it. The soil's soft.'

'What's he doing?' I asked.

'One stray thought,' said Corrie. 'So harmless. He's just invited her into his head. She was just tuned to get past his defences.'

I swore at Michael.

'Language,' said Corrie.

'Is anything actually happening down on earth?'

'We would know if it was,' said Corrie.

'Over there,' said Keziah, pointing to the horizon.

A dark cloud was boiling in the sky. As it came near, we saw that it was a swarm of imp-like, elf-like beings.

Suddenly from the tunnel, we heard a sound like rags being torn up and then army of hundreds all shouting at once.

'I think that girl was a Trojan horse,' said Jonah. 'Hundreds of them all squashed together. Michael lets in one thought and now they're swarming all over him.'

'There's a lot of these too,' said Keziah, nodding at the sky.

The swarm of imps started to land near the river, and rushed towards us, filling the ground. They were armed with bows. Others were setting up what looked like mortars. The first rounds fired, whistled over our heads and thumped into the soft earth behind.

'Okay,' said Jonah. 'There's about 10,000 of them heading towards us. Corrie—'

'I'll round up some of his best memories,' said the old lady.

'Jamie,' said Jonah, 'Help us build a big barricade. Keziah and I will hold them off. Then you go in and talk to him.'

'To Michael?'

'Yes.'

'Me?'

'Yes.'

Corrie strode towards the cathedral. A glare from her seemed enough to keep the hordes from attacking her.

'Barriers and weaponry first,' said Jonah. In the heavens we can create things by thinking about them.

I stepped back from behind the pile of dead wood, looked at it, and pasted a copy of it on the ground between us and the advancing army. When the first one worked, I repeated the thought again and then again, creating a long barrier of dead wood, starting in the middle of the field of battle and extending outwards to either side.

Keziah magicked up a helmet, breastplate and sword and took up station behind this barrier. I ran up to it, thought into being a flame thrower, and set the dry wood alight. I ran along the length of the barrier, shooting flames into the wood so the whole thing flamed.

Beyond it a legion of elves and imps was running towards us. It was, I noticed in an exhilarated moment, agreeably like a *Lord of the Rings* film.

Jonah positioned himself further along the barrier. He did not appear to have any weapons.

'I bet you can do the thing with your fingers, like the Emperor at the end of Star Wars,' I said.

'I can,' said Jonah.

The barrier burned. The imps charged. The mortars flew overhead. We waited.

'What happens if we don't stop them?' I called to Jonah.

'They overwhelm his soul. And that really will be the end of everything for him.'

'What about us?'

'We just have to live with ourselves afterwards.'

Some of the imps and elves were managing to bridge their way over the burning barricades. Others, we could see, were racing towards new tunnel entrances that had been opened when the Trojan horse girl exploded. When they reached them, they slipped off their clothes, and ran inside naked.

Keziah was swinging her sword into the imps and elves that had climbed over the barricades. They were not enjoying this. Within a few seconds a pile of dismembered spiritual beings were accumulating around her.

Each was trying to crawl away with whatever limbs were left and trying to reassemble themselves. Meanwhile nearby imps and elves were finding they had urgent appointments elsewhere.

I gave Keziah my flame-thrower.

'Welcome to the 21st century,' I said. Keziah put her sword into her belt, gave the lever a trial squeeze and watched a jet of fire burn its way into a group who were massed just outside sword range.

'Hah!' she said.

'We've got this,' called Jonah, zapping imps with lightning that flowed from his fingers. 'You go talk to Michael.'

'What shall I say?' I called.

'You'll think of something. Try and save his soul.'

'Why me?'

'You'll be good at it,' said Jonah. 'Or maybe you're the only one available.'

I turned towards the tunnel. It was getting darker overhead, a brownish, smoggy half-light: the outer limits of the Sump of Lost Dreams.

The earth all around me was spattered with the soil-splash from the mortars.

I glanced up the slope at Michael's cathedral. Its wall was leaning out towards us and bulging. Evidently the tunnels and the mortars and the acid of the Sump were undermining the cathedral's foundations.

I should have been scrambling into a tunnel but I paused to watched the cathedral wall topple over, taking with it a large piece of roof. Chunks of masonry toppled from the adjacent walls. Everything was crumbling.

*

It was warm in the tunnel, and dark. Stooping, I kicked my way through piles of earth until I came into a much wider space.

Here it was dull, red, sweaty and noisy. Years of an old man's fantasies. Naked imps and fantasy remnants were crowding around a narrower tunnel at the end.

'Is he in there?' I asked some half-clad middle-aged woman, but she ignored me. 'Look, I've got a sword-thing here. It's quite big. It might be just easier to let me through.'

'You don't want to go there,' said another female fantasy. 'That leads to the cathedral.'

'Noted. Thank you so much.' The fantasy women generally stood aside. The imps I just poked with my sword until they moved.

The new tunnel was quieter and I scrambled through it. It was very dark.

Groping along, I suddenly heard a rumble, followed by a heavy impact outside.

As if more parts of the cathedral were falling down. There was a small roof-fall and I stopped for a moment.

Not a good moment, dark tunnel, serious masonry rolling around. Suffocation. Lovely. I spat the soil out of my mouth and clawed and stumbled forward again.

The despair was everywhere, in the air. But I could see a faint glow of light in the distance.

I pushed through more collapsed soil, over a piece of masonry, and finally caught up with Michael just at the end of the tunnel. It faced out into the ruined cathedral. Michael was on his hands and knees.

'Michael,' I said. 'It's Jamie. Think of me as a voice of common sense in your head.'

'That would be novel.'

'How are you?' I asked.   I couldn't think of anything else to say.

'Angry,' said Michael. 'I'm so sick of fighting. I'm always fighting. I'm sick of it.'

'I see.'

'It will never end,' said Michael. 'I'm so tired of being a hypocrite.'

Michael pushed through the rubble and out of the collapsing tunnel. He lay on his face, breathing hard. I followed him.

'Thing I found,' I said, 'with the coma and everything.' (I actually meant, 'with Lottie and everything' but let that pass.) 'Is that it's hopeless when you look all out at the future stretching ahead of you. Nobody can face that. I'll never manage that. I decided all I can deal with is Today.'

'I've made a mess of today,' said Michael.

'Not yet you haven't,' I said. 'Well, not as much as you could yet make.'

'There's no fuel left in the tank,' said Michael, 'and I just want to give in.'

The cathedral was all around us, and there was fighting everywhere.

Jonah and Keziah must have slowly retreated into the cathedral but they were still fighting with flamethrower and lightning, trying to keep the heat off us.

Then I saw Corrie Bright walk into the cathedral from the front, at the head of a curious line, like scenes from a photo album: Michael's daughters, several copies, different sizes. Some cars that were sensible Vicar choices once, though now probably rusting on a scrapheap. Older versions of his daughters, carrying tennis equipment. And what I assumed were parishioners, bearing picnics.

'Some wonderful memories, Michael,' called out Corrie. 'And more will come. And more are still to be made.'

They deployed across the cathedral and joined the fight.

A dog started gnawing at Michael's leg.

Keziah stepped over quickly and burnt the dog's head off. The dog said 'Aww', and toppled onto the cathedral paving.

'Nice,' said Jonah, standing over Michael now, deterring further attacks.

I got down on my hands and knees next to Michael. 'Come on Michael!' I said. 'Think how near you are! All these years waiting!'

Still, imps and dogs were everywhere, and the cathedral was open to the sky, and the brown fug of the Sump of Lost Dreams was curling into his soul.

Michael crawled towards the altar, and some of his good memories reached out and pulled him along. I helped them. 'Not all days are bad days,' I said, again remembering my own illness. 'You get good days too. You can forget that in the middle of a bad day.'

The cleric lay face down on the floor, battered and bleeding, and now there was no budging him. I looked at Keziah, then at Jonah. They looked blankly back at me.

'Nothing left in the tank,' gasped Michael.

The cathedral was shattered. Memories and evil beings fought each other in the nave. Acidic brown smog thickened around us, as Michael's soul tumbled into the Sump.

Michael started to sob, not loudly, but as I looked down I could see his whole body trembling.

The brown smog thickened and we could feel it in our own spirits. The dead weight of failure; a tired anger; a cynicism; a dull feeling that we'll never escape the badness of the world and may as well get stuck in and join it.

Corrie Bright was now treading her way through the debris and joining us.

'How's the Rural Dean?' she asked Jonah.

'Broken,' said the prophet.

'We're just waiting here?' I asked, feeling gloomy about everything.

'Sometimes you do everything you can, and then see if it's enough,' said Jonah.

Suddenly, the cathedral bell sounded, a long, slow, deep *dong* that rang through the whole building, and through our spirits. The evil beings looked up, then started fighting again.

A few seconds later, another *dong*.

The beings looked at each other.

And another. Then yet another. The bell tolled, deep, relentless.

Michael became quite calm.

Still the bell kept sounding, and some of the more jittery elves and imps starting to crowd out of the building, taking wing and flying away through the soupy brown smog.

I counted twelve peals, and then everything fell silent. The demons were scattering in larger numbers. Some screamed.

A bright light from the sky pierced the brown gloom.

Magnesium white, fierce and terrible, the light grew nearer, then resolved itself into a great shining bird, all white fire, many times taller than us, and with a hooked beak like an eagle or a kestrel.

It was hovering high above.

We stepped back—everyone did—as it tucked its wings, dived, and landed with its claws either side of Michael's prone body. It steadied itself, then reached down with its beak and none-too-gently tugged at Michael's shoulder and turned him over, so that he was lying face up.

It put a clawed foot on his chest.

It carefully removed his glasses with its beak, and tossed them aside.

Then it pecked his eye out.

Michael screamed and convulsed. I gagged and almost threw up. Keeping its foot on his chest, the bird then pecked out his second eye. It tossed its feathered head, spread out its wings—the intense light from them casting shadows behind us—and with heavy beats flew back up through the roof and out of sight.

Michael's body convulsed again. Gasping for breath, he covered his eye sockets with his hands and rolled over onto his face.

I could not believe the horror of what I'd just seen.

The great bird had burned a hole in the brown smog, and around the rim more smog seemed to be dispersing. Spots of rain, fresh and golden, began to fall, further freshening us before spattering on the paving stones of the floor.

# LOST AND FOUND

'You know that I love you,' Michael whispered quietly, and not to us. He was still lying face down in front of the altar. His eyes were bleeding. 'You know, you *know*, that I love you.'

None of us said anything. The evil beings, frightened by the bell and the bird and now scalded by the rain, were dispersing fast.

'You memories,' called out Corrie briskly. 'You can go back home now.'

'I can smell something,' I said finally.

The last of the smog from the Sump of Lost Dreams was dissipating. The rain fell harder, drenching but delicious.

'We've been here before. I know this smell. It's like spring.'

Finally I saw that Michael's soul was passing nearby a great pillar in the sky.

'This is Seasons House!' I said. 'How can it be so near the Sump of Lost Dreams? How can Michael find his way when he's lying on the floor and can't see?'

Michael was slowly getting to his feet. His sightless eyes would not have spotted the pillars of Seasons House, but perhaps his nose picked up the scents.

'I can make a phone call,' Michael said to himself, with a voice light with the simplicity of it all. 'I can make a simple phone call and all this will go away. All

I've got to do is just quietly sort out the problem. Vulnerable girl in house. Get help. Huh.'

A few moments later, on earth, Keziah's phone started ringing.

*

Michael was already at Madge's when I arrived the next morning. I hung up my coat, fired up the computer and started feeding and tending the coffee machine.

'What a night!' said Michael.

'How do you mean?' I asked, feigning surprise.

'Terrible. I was woken by a hammering on my door. One of my customers from the café. Sixteen-year-old girl. Wanted somewhere to stay.

'I've plenty of rooms of course, so I cooked her a snack and put her up in a spare bedroom, made sure she was all right.

'But I could hear after half an hour she hadn't settled and was very disturbed. She was calling for me. And I suspected from her eyes and because I knew her history that she was fond of methamphetamines and alcohol.'

'And you'd rather be tucked up reading the *Church Times*.'

'I sort-of snapped to my senses and realized how vulnerable she was.'

'You both.'

'I suppose. What could I do? I did know one person who is good with teenage girls, available at a moment's notice and likely to forgive me for phoning her at three in the morning. Our lawyer friend Keziah.'

'You phoned Keziah?'

'She claimed she was awake anyway and had been already working. Strange. She came over. When I told my guest what was happening she became even more disturbed and angry. So when Keziah arrived I left them to it, slipped out and came here.'

'You spent the night here?'

'Yes.'

'I thought you hadn't shaved.'

'Indeed I missed my morning mow. Keziah settled her down and she's taking her to the Women's Centre when it opens this morning. That young woman is a treasure.'

'She comes wrapped in barbed wire, though.' I said. 'Where's Mark by the way?'

'He's seeing a property lawyer with the Chapel trustees. It seems all the ducks are finally in place.' Michael was seated at his desk with his cup of hot water and fairly traded dead leaves. His eyes were bright. 'If we get planning permission today, Mark wants to exchange contracts tomorrow.'

'Remind me why you can't just buy it outright now?'

'Would be nice,' said Michael. 'But without planning permission we can't get both sides of the equation to match.'

'We haven't got enough money.'

'Yes. As you know the deal is that we buy the chapel. Then the trustees settle their debts and give out some gifts. And then they a give a sum to us, and we pay off our loan. So all we have to do is borrow some money for about a week, which Mark is fine with.'

'Why don't they just sell us the Chapel very cheaply, save all the bother.'

'Tax,' said Michael. 'Elspeth wants to pay it.'

'She wants to pay tax.'

'Correct. She doesn't want a whiff of tax-dodging. She wants to do it right.'

'So we buy it at a fair price, they take the money, and then give most of it back. Minus the tax, but still a big gift. That's nice of them.'

'They believe in us.'

'Don't they need a church of their own any more?'

'Elspeth is the youngest member of the congregation, aged 87. She is preparing her congregation to unite with the Reformed Baptists across town, who are not Strict but are apparently, sufficiently Particular.'

'Is she growing liberal in her old age?'

'I think they've forgotten what they disagreed over.'

'And it is all legal?'

'Seems so. So long as The Oyster Café and the Chapel have compatible aims, they can sell it to us for whatever they like. It seems the Strict and Particular Baptist Trust document is vague enough to include our proposed Oyster Cafe.

'Of course it all works a lot better when we have planning permission. Actually, the same goes for all our grant applications.'

'So it could all be sorted out this week or next?'

'Yes.'

'Mark doesn't seem too stressed anyway.'

'I think he likes it.'

'And you? — I mean it's still all uncertain, isn't it? Grants, money, getting it off the ground. Now being assailed by drug-crazed young women. Must be stressful.'

Michael hesitated, and took a sip of tea.

'You're not—especially—as I understand it—forgive me if I'm wrong—a person of a particularly active Christian praxis.'

These clerics are scrupulous not to offend but I understood he was calling me a great hairy unwashed pagan.

'I give some money every year to Kidney Research. I'm not sure if that counts.'

'I'm sure that will stand you in good stead on the Great Day of Judgement,' said Michael. But he clearly wanted to say something else. 'So—am I stressed? Quite the opposite.'

It was true. His eyes said as much. 'It has been an extraordinary night. Does the name Blaise Pascal mean anything to you?'

I flipped though my mental Wikipedia. 'Er—was he something to do with pressure? Or triangles?'

'French mathematician,' said Michael.

'Not his fault he was French.'

'Indeed.'

'Though he could have renounced it, I suppose. You might be born French but you don't have to stay French.'

'Anyway,' insisted Michael, with the slightly wearied air of the model-maker whose train keeps falling off the tracks, 'he was a sporadically religious Roman Catholic. One night he had an intense experience of God. It totally changed him. After that he became a zealous apologist. He wrote a contemporary note of the experience which he sewed into his clothes. Pascal always carried it with him. A servant found it when he died. Do you know what it said?'

'No.'

'*Fire*. That was the start anyway.'

'Have you heard of Thomas Aquinas?'

'Don't think so.'

'One of the Roman Catholics' Doctors of the Church. There aren't that many.'

'Rock-star theologians.'

'In a manner of speaking.'

'Theological problems and existential angst our speciality. No dilemma too big or small.'

'Aquinas wrote a great synthesis of Christian doctrine and Greek Philosophy that set the tone of the Western church in the Middle Ages.'

'I suppose it's a way of passing the time.'

'Near the end of his life, he too had an extraordinary experience. Unlike Pascal, who started writing, Aquinas stopped. He could write no more. All he'd ever written couldn't do justice to what he'd suddenly experienced.'

'This is going somewhere?'

'Something like that happened to me.'

'Really?'

'Last night. With a vulnerable, drug-crazy youngster yammering my name and hammering on the wall.'

'OK.'

'Something happened. In all that. I don't know. The upshot is, the more lost I feel, the more found I feel. The more blind I am, the more I can see.'

'If you say so.'

'So in all the uncertainty and hope, somehow, I don't worry. Does that make any sense?'

'Honestly not,' I said.

'Well never mind.'

'I'm happy for you though.'

'Thank you.'

# THE DECISION

The planning committee meeting was scheduled at 2:00pm at the council offices not so far from us.

Mark returned around 11:30, his usual bright self, and dropped into his chair. Michael was downstairs, organising his twice-weekly cafe at Madge's.

'One last spanner in the works,' Mark told me. 'Those developers have sent an offer to buy the Chapel. Offering stupid money. More than us. And their plans are being considered along with ours.'

'Can they do that?'

'Yes. And we've no idea whether or not there's funny stuff going on in planning.

'*And* they also faxed our solicitor claiming that the trustees were legally bound to accept the highest offer, and that they were willing to fight that in court.'

'But our lawyers disagree with them?'

'Yes. We believe the trustees can dispose of the property to a like-minded group for whatever price they like.'

'And our lawyers are bigger and uglier than their lawyers?'

'Yes. The snag is that the developers have a lot more money than we have. They are gambling that we will settle and concede rather than expensively fight them in court.'

'Why would we do that?'

'Because the trustees would end up getting more money for the chapel. A lot more if there aren't court costs to pay. Which the trustees can give to us if they want. And we can build our Oyster Cafe somewhere else.'

'But not in a prime city site?'

'No.'

'Which is useless for the Oyster Café?'

'Yes. So the whole project will flop,' said Mark.

'Seems like very bad luck,' I said.

'Everything's public domain,' said Mark. 'So in one sense it's not surprising … You're not wrong though. The initial refusal, the press attention, now this. You could feel that somebody, somewhere doesn't like us.'

'A hidden mole in the planning department.'

'I thought all moles were hidden. That's the nature of a mole.'

'OK. A mole in the planning department.'

'Planning dastardly deeds. Definitely. Oh, there's another thing. Even more important. Don't tell anyone. The chapel has no buildings insurance.'

'What?' I said.

'Yeah. Elspeth told me. It lapsed a month ago and they didn't renew it because it was an annual policy and they expected the building to be long sold by then.'

'No buildings insurance at all?' I gaped. I am from an insurance dynasty. As a child, I had lived many years before I first touched an uninsured object. (Apart from my sisters obviously.) Mum, Dad, home, dog, holidays, all were cocooned in policies and usually with no-claims bonuses as well. Insurance even prices in 'Acts of God'. Insurance *rocks*.

'The Lord has looked after the building since 1874, apparently,' continued Mark, 'and it was felt He could manage it on his own for a few weeks.'

'Aren't you worried?'

'It's less than totally ideal. At least we know our first job after exchanging contracts tomorrow.'

Mark went to the planning meeting and Michael planned to join him as soon as the temporary Oyster Cafe was cleared up downstairs. I'd chosen to stay in the office.

Something was nagging at my mind. But I couldn't figure what it was.

*

Mark phoned at 4:30.

'The meal's on,' he said. 'Common sense prevailed over the forces of anarchy.'

'We got permission?'

'We got permission.'

'What about the other developers?'

'They have outline permission.'

'Are they going to fight us in court?'

'We are going to exchange contracts and hope they go away.'

'So we did it.'

'We did.'

# NOT A DAMP SQUIB

That night's celebratory meal, in a restaurant that looked down on the river from three storeys, didn't go too well.

It was satisfying to toast the new Oyster Cafe, the first project spawned by Mark's social enterprise fund—a Cambridge double first. Despite all the obstacles, we had navigated it safely through the birth canal. We'd got permission to convert the Strict and Particular Baptist Chapel into a hub for the homeless. Tomorrow we could exchange contracts—hastily buy some buildings insurance—and move on to the next milestone.

In the heavenlies, Leopold had tried and failed to destroy me, and Michael and even perhaps Lottie. He had not seemingly got anywhere near Mark's or Keziah's defences. So he had lost, and presumably was due further career trouble, perhaps a demotion back to the Complaints Department of Pandemonium.

But even with all that, the proposed Oyster Cafe CEO (Michael), the chair (Mark), the comms person (me) and the first customer for the office space (Keziah) weren't your perfect blend for a fizzing dinner party.

Michael had a quarter of a century over the rest of us, and he was clubbable enough. The real distraction wasn't even Mark's obvious infatuation for Keziah. It was that the lawyer appeared to have spent the last several hours inside her fridge.

She was normally rude, difficult and truculent, but this evening, the hour of our victory, she was unearthing fresh depths.

And especially to Mark, her alleged boyfriend, whom she seemed to regard more like something you stepped in than someone you fell in love with.

Michael and I left after coffee, while Keziah and Mark seemed keen to stay on, order more coffee. Clearly negotiations had to be had.

I couldn't imagine this was going to end well.

What was this impossible person doing? How hard was it for one night—the night we'd all won—just to behave like a decent human?

I tumbled into bed with plenty on my mind. And just beyond the realms of conscious thought, something was nagging at me.

*

When you're asleep, your spirit wanders around your soul. Often it's tidying up. Sometimes it's cleaning.

Just occasionally it stumbles over something so alarming that it stops and wakes the soul up. *This*, it seems to judge, *can't wait.*

Something like that happened to me that night.

From the depths of a warm and occasionally snorting slumber, I jerked straight upright in bed, paused for a moment for the blood to refill my head, then reached for my phone, and squinted at the time.

4:13am.

Without thinking about the time, or what may have gone on between Mark and Keziah after we'd left them, or any of the consequences, I poked at Keziah's name on my phone.

Keziah answered after a couple of rings and inquired with forthrightness why I chose to honour her with a call.

'You know the chapel was all over the news this last week because of the fuss that Julian caused.'

'Yes,' said Keziah.

'And your arsonist friend Derek O'Malley is still sleeping on the streets?'

'Yes.'

'And Leopold might still be unfolding plans against us?'

'Yes.'

'Have you ever put these things together? Leopold. Derek. Chapel. Big empty building full of wooden pews. Arsonist. Publicity. Leopold playing on people's minds. What does your friend Derek do with big empty buildings full of wood that are in the news? What might he do with a bit of prodding?'

There was a silence at the other end of the phone, followed by a one-phrase summary of our position.

'It's worse,' I said. 'Mark told me that the chapel has no fire insurance.'

'We should go to the chapel,' said Keziah.

'Shouldn't we tell Jonah and Corrie Bright?'

'We can do that once we're there.'

We finished our call but I was still dressing when the phone lit up again.

'Mark,' I said. 'I didn't know you got up this early.'

'I'm sorry to wake you, Jamie,' he said. His voice was a little shaky. I thought you'd want to know. You don't need to come, but I'm at the chapel. I got a call from Elspeth. She heard from the fire brigade. Someone's set it on fire.'

*

Michael, Elspeth, Keziah and I all joined Mark at about the same time. I'd cycled, but they'd parked their cars crazily on the pavements, with no regard for residents' parking restrictions.

We were part of a small crowd of neighbours and clubbers, standing in the deserted Mill Road, safely ushered from the main action by a fire person. We saw three engines, heavy hoses snaking over the pavement, fire fighters plodding around in wellies, the whole scene lit by the flames and by flashing blue.

Half the roof was gone. The windows were empty. Flames and sparks curled into the night. The five of us were standing together, a little away from the other onlookers. No-one was speaking. Mark and Keziah were standing far apart from each other, at the opposite ends of our group.

'My business is in there,' said Keziah, looking at the smoke.

'You've got a backup, I suppose.'

'Not the handwritten stuff, which is most of it.'

Keziah's phone rang and after a brief conversation she clicked it off.

'That was Derek O'Malley,' she said to me, and explained to the others, 'a friend of mine. He handed himself in at the police station and he wants me to be there for the interview. He's going to confess to burning the chapel down.'

'A friend of yours,' said Mark, with some exasperation.

'What if he is?' spat Keziah.

'Can't you control these people?' Mark sounded uncharacteristically peevish.

'These *people* are the ones we've set this cafe up for, and no, I can't control them,' snapped Keziah. 'Some people can't just be manoeuvred around like little puppets.'

She rushed off and Michael and I exchanged glances.

There didn't seem to be anything else to say, so we went back to watching the blaze.

The chief fire person, who was middle aged and overweight but clearly enjoyed a good crisis, told us it was well under control and that they hoped it would be damped down soon enough. TV crews and reporters arrived, vans further cluttering the pavements.

Mark had been unusually silent and still as he stood watching the flames. He glanced at Elspeth, Michael and me in turn.

'What's left,' he said coolly, 'will be an unusable, unstable building and some expensive land. Expensive to demolish. What's going up in smoke is our chance to run the Oyster Café. I'm really sorry.'

Michael briefly put an arm round his shoulder.

'However we string it together,' Mark went on, 'We haven't enough money for a new-build. We were hoping just to move in.'

'I'm so sorry,' said Elspeth. 'It's all my fault.'

'You didn't burn it down,' said Michael.

'I didn't look after it,' said Elspeth. 'All these years. I didn't steward it properly right at the end.'

'You didn't have a lot of support,' I suggested.

'I didn't do what I was supposed to do,' insisted Elspeth. 'I failed the Lord.'

I couldn't help wishing the Lord had covered for her this once, after she'd faithfully covered for him all these years.

'It's not the end for you,' said Mark. 'The site's still worth money. Someone will have to make the site good, pull the chapel down, build something new. You'll still end up in profit. You can pay off all your bills and still give some money away.'

'But no Oyster Café,' said Michael.

'I'm so sorry,' said Mark.

# DESTROYER OF WORLDS

The sky was still inky November dark when the fire officer in charge told us that they had successfully damped down the building, and that perhaps we ought to order a security firm to keep the site safe. He showed Mark a few numbers on his phone.

Elspeth also made to go. 'I ought to go back and feed Mephibosheth,' she said. 'He'll be outside, mewing.'

'Not a boyfriend?' I said.

'Cat,' she said.

'Easier,' I agreed.

Michael offered to give her a ride back, which left just Mark and I.

*

'There's a café down there,' I pointed down Mill Road. 'Opens early and does these big bacon bap things.'

'I don't think I'm hungry,' said Mark.

'That's what everybody says,' I replied. 'Until they see one.'

'A cup of tea at least wouldn't go amiss,' said Mark, who looked rather dazed.

*

The café was warm, already busy, and with steamed-up windows. Most people, it seemed, were talking about the fire. I weaved through the noisy tables carefully carrying a tray to where Mark had taken a seat. 'This is the light option,' I told him, passing him a white bap, six inches in diameter, stuffed with bacon and bubbling with tomato.

They also did giant mugs of tea, and I passed his to him and took my seat.

I took my first bite and followed it with a slurp of tea.

'Much better,' I said once it had all gone down. 'My face was warm with the fire but my feet are freezing. I suppose on average you would say I should be just nicely warm. You look awful.'

It was true. Mark was pale, unshaven, and his eyes were tired and full of pain.

I took another bite and another drink. 'How bad is it?'

Mark took a small bite and a longer drink of tea.

'It's Michael I feel for,' he said. 'He'd invested so much hope in the project.'

'Yeah, but he seems robust. But you look like someone's pierced a hole in you and drained all your juice out. I recommend more bacon and tea. I guess you've lost a lot of money? I'm sorry.'

Mark took another polite bite, no way to tackle this kind of food. You have to run at a bacon bap of this magnitude if you are to have any hope of successfully downing it all. But I let that pass.

'Money comes and goes in my experience,' he said. 'In my old job we lost more projects than we won.'

He drew with his finger on the café table, not a good idea, ploughing through years of congealed fat and dust. 'That's not actually my main problem tonight.'

'It's not?'

'No,' he said.

'Golly,' I whistled. 'What could be worse than this?'

'A lawyer,' he said.

'Any lawyer?' I asked.

'No, a particular lawyer.'

Which being interpreted means that sometime last night Keziah had jumped on his heart with her heavy boots and pulverised it and kicked the bits into a dustbin.

And then she's probably done the same with her own.

Project 'K' on his soul had backfired. Or blown up. And sunk him.

'Mark,' I said. 'I'm really sorry.'

*

We each went to our homes and I stood under the shower for a long time, trying to wash out the smell of fire, the ash, the sense of not having slept, and what can only be described as cold fury against a member of the legal profession.

Keziah Mordant, destroyer of worlds, I have had enough of you.

After I dressed, I phoned Keziah.

'Where are you?'

'I'm in what's left of my office in the chapel,' said Keziah. 'Trying to find what hasn't been destroyed.'

'Is that safe?''

'The back didn't burn so much and the fire people said it was OK.'

'Is Mark with you?'

'No. Why should he be?'

'I'm coming over,' I said.

*

I cycled back to Mill Road, which the fire service had reopened. The street had repopulated itself effortlessly with cars, bikes, delivery vans, people carrying boxes, people with shopping bags or strollers or dogs or all three.

The remains of the Strict and Particular Baptist Chapel were fenced off now by red plastic netting and traffic cones and guarded by two burly men in high-vis jackets, who were eating pies.

I explained who I was and they sent me down a small alley to the side. Keziah had set up her space some weeks ago in the disused church office. Apparently this room was still structurally OK, despite being trashed by smoke and water and the fire service.

The door was open and I stepped inside.

'Hello,' I said. 'I brought coffee, though it's a bit refined for you.'

The little lawyer was kneeling and sorting through a heap of files, saving some and evidently discarding others as too water-damaged to read. She smiled briefly.

That made me worry she really was losing her grip.

'I can't get my laptop to work,' she said.

'Is it charged?' I asked.

'Yes.'

'It might just need to dry out. Do you want me to have a go?'

'Feel free.'

'Water doesn't always do a lot of damage. Not to keyboards, for example. Don't know about smoke though.'

I fiddled a bit with the laptop, not getting any life.

'It was Derek?' I asked.

'Yes.'

'Why?'

'He doesn't know.'

'What will happen to him?'

'He'll probably go down for a long time, even if Elspeth tries to mitigate for him. We might be able to get him in a secure hospital.'

'Is that better?' I said.

'He doesn't have a lot of choices,' said Keziah.

'Nothing from this laptop by the way. You've got a backup offsite?'

'Some,' she said. 'But a lot was handwritten, all the notes on the files.'

It was gloomy in the powerless office, of course, and she was crouched inelegantly as she sifted paper. Even allowing for all that, she looked spent and numb.

I tugged at my earlobe, and took a breath in, and scratched my nose.

'I'm going to tell you something.' I said. 'It's important. I might even ask you to put the files down.'

I joined her, kneeling on the floor.

'Don't worry, nothing bad's going to happen,' I said. 'It's nearly a year since you crashed into me. Thanks to you I lost my job, my health and my girlfriend (though possibly she'd already gone by that time). I lost my *life*, which was a nice life. You put me in a coma and I had to fight all the way back to health, and I've shed a lot of tears, and then I've had to work with you and you are a short-tempered pain in the bum with all the tenderness of the 101st Airborne Division.'

'And you're not exactly—'

'I haven't finished. Along with you I've been doing the soul work which is messy and often tragic and because of that I have made the uncomfortable discovery that I am self-centered, lazy, greedy, callous and unfeeling. Possibly even more than you. And that was why Lottie left me. And I've learnt that fixing all this is very painful and perhaps impossible. I still haven't finished—'

'I was going to add chauvinistic and pig-headed,' added Keziah.

'Fair point. Forgot these,' I said. 'But I still wanted to say two things. Number one. Thank you for crashing into me last January. I am totally at sea and unhappy a lot of the time but it's wonderful. I've wanted to say that for a long time. I wouldn't go back. I'm not exactly sure why but I wouldn't go back. I've found something Keziah. If only I knew what it was. And some of that—not much of it, but some of it—is due to working with you.

'You were very slightly good for me. It is possible you may be very slightly good for other people as well.' I had some tears in my eyes now. I squished them with a few blinks. 'Which takes me to the second thing. What have you done to Mark Bright?'

Keziah opened her little mouth. 'Shut up. I haven't finished. If you don't make peace with that man and give him hope that one day you and he might come to something, or that at least you *might* come to something, then you are the most bone-headed, emotionally crippled waste of space I've ever met. Without wanting to point things out too starkly.

'I am now going to hug you by way of thanks and forgiveness which is going to be embarrassing for both of us and then I am going to leave you and you are going to sort yourself out.

'We need to get this over with.'

It was a terrible hug, one-sided, stiff, difficult because we were both kneeling on the floor, awkward as we determinedly avoided any face-contact and generally the kind of thing you never do again.

Then I left.

The security guards had finished their pies. It was sunny in Mill Road. I passed couples, the girls in black leggings and neat short skirts, teasing and poking their boyfriends as they argued animatedly down the street.

# THE LAWYER AND THE SUMP

On a whim, I turned my bike away from Madge's, where I had been heading, and cycled to one of the large Georgian houses near the centre. Here the University housed the still-breathing relics of Corrie Bright, physicist and soul maven.

I locked my bike to her railings, climbed the steps, rang the doorbell, and heard her call me in.

I had visited Corrie in the flesh before and so I was prepared, as I walked down her hall, for the odd smells in the living room, and her blotched hairy face. She was sitting frail and upright in her winged armchair, with a pile of academic reading and a beer on the table to her side.

'Hello Corrie,' I said, stooping to kiss her. 'I don't know how much news you've heard.'

'I had to sneak back to my body so my carer didn't think I had finally slipped the bonds. I think I heard most of it from the gossipers. Leopold is busy composing a report for his superiors. Apparently he's already thinking of developing a training course and marketing it through Pandemonium.'

'I can't believe this,' I said. 'Leopold has taken out Derek, the Oyster Café, Keziah and Mark, all in a single night. It's a disaster.'

'I don't know. I think the whole project is in much better shape,' said Corrie.

'The Oyster Cafe's off. It's not going to happen.'

'Not in its current form. But think about what else has happened. Look at Michael.'

'Well he was attacked and barely rescued. Then he had that experience—'

'Which settled his soul at last,' said Corrie.

'I suppose.'

'If he hadn't suffered that terrible attack, it wouldn't have happened. And what about you?'

'I was just talking to Keziah. I told her that thanks to her I was completely broken and wrecked but all the better for it. I know it's true, but I don't know why.'

'You were broken before, but you never knew it. Now you know you are, that's progress. When did it happen?'

'In stages. So I take your point partly. But I've just seen both Mark and Keziah and both of them look like Stub on a really bad run.'

'Unfortunately true,' said Corrie. 'Both their souls have fallen into the Sump of Lost Dreams.'

'Because of last night?'

'Yes, but it was before the fire.'

'Let me guess. Mark said one loving thing to Keziah, made one effort to reach out to her, and she tore his head off and spat in the hole?'

'That would be my guess also.'

'And he loves her.'

'I think so.'

'I've just been over and told Keziah she's a moron.'

'Did that help?'

'Certainly helped me.'

'I think our dear friend panicked,' said Corrie. 'Plus she's exhausted.'

'And when Keziah has a strong emotional reaction—'

'Yes. There's a body count.'

'Can we do anything about it?'

'What do you think?' asked Corrie.

'I'm think I'm totally out of my depth. I thought I could do something with Lottie and I was completely wrong.'

'Indulge an old woman anyway,' said Corrie.

'I think Keziah needs throttling,' I said. 'She's hurting Mark, and herself, and all because she's scared.

'It's not like Lottie, who maybe just needs time. Keziah doesn't need time. I'm not even sure she's *got* time. I did try telling her but of course I made sure I left the room as soon as possible afterwards.'

'I think you coming here was a good idea,' said Corrie.

'Hang on a second,' I said, spotting the mischief in her eye. 'Where did that idea come from?'

'From your own intrinsic good nature, I expect,' said Corrie sweetly.

'The idea that I should come and talk to a rascally old woman who plots things? And drops ideas into souls?'

'A splendid idea of yours Jamie,' said Corrie. 'Just what I'd expect.'

'I think,' I said, 'if you're not waiting for any visitors, I should sit in this sofa, and you in your chair, and maybe we should go visit Keziah.'

'What an excellent idea,' said Corrie. 'Your soul has a cricket pitch?'

'It does.'

'I'll meet you there, and I'll bring a chariot.'

*

Corrie and I took the chariot through the heavens toward the bromide river which smoked and spat its way through the garish carnival of Vanity Fair.

Corrie got the pengub to start descending.

We sank into the Sump of Lost Dreams, first feeling wisps of gloom and despondency, then sudden spasms of melancholy. The lights above us became blurred by the soupy brown mist and I felt a coldness settle on my spirit.

We passed a hideous, rotted skeletal soul to our right, a ghost-soul.

'Is that person dead?' I asked.

'Technically not,' said Corrie. 'They might still have their own TV show, for all I know, and legions of fans. But it's only a matter of time.'

I shivered.

'There's Mark,' said Corrie, pointing out the venture capitalist's yacht-like soul below us and to our left. Its sail was drooping and the line connecting it to its pengub was slack.

'It doesn't look too badly damaged,' I suggested.

'The Sump's insidious,' said Corrie. 'The longer you're here, the more you rot.'

'I seemed to get out fairly easily.'

'You weren't there long and it's a lot easier. Plus if I may say so, you're not the world's most sensitive person, so you have a level of natural immunity.'

We floated on, past several more beleaguered souls.

'I recognise him!' I pointed Corrie to a small city-like soul. 'That's Julian Faber, the planner. What's he doing here?'

'A triumph,' said Corrie. 'Hard on him.'

'Shouldn't we do something for him?'

'I don't think we can. Maybe one day. There's our legal eagle.'

Corrie pointed out Keziah's soul which seemed to have come to a halt in the Sump of Lost Dreams. Corrie took us into a gentle landing in a hidden fold of rocks high in Keziah's volcanic mountain range.

We climbed out and looked over toward the pointy end of her soul.

The pot-bound silver birch was enormous, hundreds of feet high. It stood next to Keziah's scar, perhaps a kilometre from us. It was surrounded by a vast pile of rocks, gently glowing blue. Sitting on the rocks was someone who looked like Keziah.

'Which one's that?' I whispered to Corrie Bright.

'Given that the real Keziah is occupied in her office, and that one is carrying a machine gun, and that it appears to have conquered her soul, I would say that's the alt-Keziah.'

'I'm going to see her,' I told Corrie Bright.

'I think I'll come too,' said Corrie.

We hiked down the mountain. When the alt-Keziah saw me, she stood up and pointed her weapon.

I kept walking. 'You've shot me before and it doesn't work,' I called. 'Apparently I'm too emotionally vacuous.'

'Won't work on me either,' said Corrie. 'Too cranky.' Alt-Keziah put her gun down.

'Why can't you leave Keziah alone?' I asked.

'Because I'm part of her!' spat alt-Keziah. 'Why can't *hope* leave her alone?'

'Look where you've brought her,' I said. 'The Sump.'

'You don't escape,' said Alt-Keziah. 'You never escape when you've been abused. You always come here.'

I started clearing the rocks away, lifting them one at a time and throwing them into the scar. Each rock was warm, and wriggled, and each time I touched one, I felt a stab of caution.

'I know what these are!' I exclaimed. 'This is Pixelated Fear! Leopold used to line our cage with it.'

Pixelated Fear, which comes in various colours, roams in herds through the heavens. Like many herds, they are easily led.

'You've been talking to Leopold!' I said to the alt -Keziah. 'He supplied all this.'

'He did. They like it here. And it's no good just throwing them away. They'll just come crawling back.'

I threw another one away. 'Not if I attack the problem at the roots,' I said. 'Corrie, can you help me? I want to clear a path through to the silver birch.'

'I'll get a little digger,' said Corrie.

'It won't work,' said alt-Keziah.

'Let me try first,' I said.

Alt-Keziah made a be-my-guest gesture and folded her arms, still sitting on the great pile of Pixelated Fear that surrounded the pot containing the silver birch.

Corrie and I dug.

These weren't happy moments. The noxious Sump crept into my spirit. Each time I picked up a piece of rock I felt a stab of anxiety. Some of the rocks we cleared came crawling back.

But still we cut a path through to the cast-iron pot that contained the vast, overgrown birch tree.

'If I can smash this open,' I said to Corrie Bright 'I think we can solve everything. Give Mark his rightful place in her heart.'

The alt-Keziah did not seem worried.

'I find a lot of things are solved with a sledgehammer,' I said.

With Pixelated Fear piled shoulder-high around me, and me standing next to the cast-iron pot, while Corrie drove up and down with her digger keeping the path clear, I magicked up a sledgehammer. It was a serious sledgehammer, the kind of thing a Nordic god like Thor might fetch from the garage if he was determined about an ironmongery job.

'Are you safe with that thing?' called out Corrie.

'Doubt it,' I said.

I could hardly lift it. But I took a good grip, clenched my teeth together, and swung the hammer horizontally, aiming straight for the cast-iron.

I had quite a momentum going and when the pot refused to crumble it was a surprise, both to me and the sledgehammer.

The energy had to go somewhere and it seemed to be shared between the most enormous *dong* that echoed through the Sump of Lost Dreams and a set of vibrations that headed towards my arms.

I dropped the hammer and flexed my jaw to confirm it hadn't been put out.

'How do you think that went?' I asked Corrie after the resonances through my bones had diminished.

But we heard a shriek from the rough direction of the cottage.

The real Keziah had evidently felt the impact, jumped over to her soul, and lost her temper, all in the same moment. She was running across the landscape towards us. 'What?—oh hello Corrie. I didn't see you there.'

'We thought we'd both come,' said Corrie Bright gently.

Keziah seemed momentarily lost for words, emotions piling up in her face like a crashing train. She was quite used to roughing me up, but Corrie was her friend and mentor. Keziah stopped her stride across the moorland and folded her arms. Alt-Keziah stood up and faced her.

'Do you know where you are?' Corrie called out to her. Keziah glanced at the bromine sky.

'Yeah, well.'

'Do you know where Mark is?'

'No.'

'Same place.'

'Too bad.'

'I don't know if you've noticed,' I said airily. 'There's an enormous tree growing in the middle of your soul all bound up in a pot. Laden with fruit. Surprising for a silver birch. Oh look, there's a label. *Mark Bright.* Does that mean anything to you?'

Standing alone in the moorland across from us, Keziah suddenly looked a little lost.

'I'm keeping him safe.'

The Pixellated Fear oozed back all around the tree.

'He's in the Sump of Lost Dreams, Keziah. That worked well then.'

'I'd worked it out,' said Keziah. 'What was the biggest threat to Mark? What was the one thing? Me. Loving me. That was his one vulnerability. It was the one thing Leopold could use to get at Mark. So I stopped him.'

'Does the word "Bonehead" mean anything to you? Like do people call you it ever?'

Keziah said nothing.

'Have you looked at your soul? Do you see what's piled up here? I think it might be an infestation of

Pixelated Fear,' I said. 'Look at it. Now. Who do you think might be responsible for a swarm of Pixelated Fear landing on your soul? Try to think Keziah.'

'Mark was vulnerable.'

'Leopold poured in the fear and you, Bonehead, lapped it up.'

Keziah looked at the piles of fear, and at the tall tree labelled Mark Bright, in its cast-iron pot.

A long silence fell.

'I tried smashing the pot,' I said. 'Hurt my elbow a bit actually.'

More Pixelated Fear climbed out of the scar in Keziah's landscape and rejoined the pile.

'Well, Bonehead, are you going to do anything about it?'

'Just everybody go away.'

'OK,' I said.

'On second thoughts, you may as well stay.'

'OK,'

'Or go, stay, I don't care.'

'OK.'

She looked so worn down.

She rested her lips against the back of the hand, almost chewing her own knuckles. Finally she put her hands on her hips and stood motionless with her head down, shoulders slumped.

I glanced at Corrie Bright who was standing impassively, thumbs tapping slowly against each other. Her bright eyes were unreadable.

'I mean, you've already lost everything,' I said. 'Leopold got you proper.'

Keziah looked up and stared at the pile of Pixellated Fear. Her hands tightened into fists.

The ground shook, hard, like someone shaking out a cloth, such that we nearly lost our balance. One of the volcanoes on the end of her soul boiled over, then another, then another. Finally they were all firing, launching rocks into the sky, issuing clouds of smoke, leaking lava.

Stones pattered around us and smoke drifted towards us. The lava poured in streams which joined up. Some poured into the scar on her soul, others made channels through the moorland and off the edge.

Slowly the smoke thinned, the lava slowed, and the volcanoes grew quiet.

It fell silent.

Keziah walked over and kicked one of the Pixellated Fears straight into her scar. Bending down, she picked up an armful and one by one flung them away. Then she started stamping on them. Some she kicked, some she threw, some she crushed.

When a soul's owner starts acting, it's powerful.

The Pixellated Fear retreated, slowly at first but getting faster. Then things became a rout, and finally a stampede.  One half of them dived into the scar. The rest flowed over the edge of her soul and into the Sump of Lost Dreams.

Keziah looked Alt-Keziah in the eye. 'Not today. Not here. Not now.'

Alt-Keziah didn't break the gaze.

'I'll never leave you,' she said. 'I'll always be close and I'll always come back.'

'Just go,' said Keziah.

'Darkness,' said Alt-Keziah, climbing down into the scar. 'So much. In the night you won't want the day to come and in the daytime you won't want the night to come.'

The squeaking, twittering, flicking noise of the fleeing Pixellated Fear died away as the last of them departed, and Keziah's soul was silent once more.

Keziah looked the tree up and down. It was impossibly large and still in its pot, top heavy, precarious.

She clenched her fists again, then unclenched them, then her head drooped, like the batteries on her had run out.

She walked towards the pot, It looked like she was walking in high gravity, heavy legs. She rested her hands on the rim of the pot.

I don't think I'd ever seen anyone so frightened, and there was no Pixellated Fear in sight.

'I won't do it,' said Keziah.

'Bonehead,' I said.

'You can make bad decisions,' said Keziah. 'You can make bad decisions that change everything and hurt people.'

'You don't need Alt-Keziah,' I told her. 'You can do it all yourself. Why don't you just *think* for once, for a change? Was the Oyster Cafe a bad decision? Mark lost thousands. Michael sunk his heart and soul into something that won't now happen. Did they get hurt? Yes. Would they do it again? Yes. Why? Because it was a wrong decision? If it was a wrong decision it was a wrong decision in the right direction. So there was both lots of risk and no risk at all. Not with a Censer above us. The real risk would have not been risking.'

Keziah looked at me.

'Finished?'

'Pretty much.'

'Good.' She then swore at me, not just once, but a lot, and ranging imaginatively through my character and works.

I took this, overall, as a good sign. Comfort cursing. The volcanoes joined in.

When it all died away again, Keziah was still resting her hands on the rim of the pot.

She looked the great tree up and down again.

She walked round it.

She looked it up and down again.

With a groan of pain, she pushed the pot.

## MADGE'S

The tree's fall was sweet and unhurried. It swung easily through the sky and crashed gently into the ground, raising a cloud of dust and twigs.

The pot crumbled, exposing a tangle of white roots which tenderly started to explore the moorland.

The tree itself seemed to have broken into many pieces. As we watched, each broken branch slowly righted itself, put down roots, and became a little sapling. The roots yielded further baby trees.

After a few minutes all the motion had ceased. The central trunk still lay across her landscape, and all over the plateau, green, fragile little saplings had appeared.

Keziah watched it silently.

'That's done it,' I said.

'Yeah,' she said.

We felt a tug on the landscape, and behind us, we could see that Keziah's pengub's reins had tightened.

'Must have smelled something,' said Corrie. 'I think Jamie and I will be off.'

Corrie Bright and I emerged back in our bodies in Corrie's apartment.

'Well that was fun,' I said to Corrie. 'A good idea of mine.'

'Indeed.'

'I think I might just cycle over to Madge's, see what's what.'

*

Mark was alone in the office when I pushed through the door. He was looking out of a tiny window, which was single-glazed and dusty and had a view of a badly-built sixteenth-century wall.

'You OK?' I asked. 'You had coffee?'

'No.'

'You need coffee?'

'Yes.'

'I'll put some on.' I put off my coat and set to work.

'I think we've done all the immediate things,' said Mark, taking his gaze away from the window. 'I've given some statements to the press. I don't know if we shouldn't work on a release for more general use.'

'We can do that,' I said. 'I'll have to update the website too, though I'm not sure with what.'

'Yes.'

'I thought I might try honesty. Say something about the chapel being burnt down and us rethinking our options. I'll show it you before we go live.'

'Sounds like a plan.'

I fiddled with the machine some more.

'OK, frothed milk, here we go.'

I made the coffee.

We set down to work.

After about half an hour the door pushed open and Keziah walked in, buried in her trench coat and carrying her huge lawyer's bag.

'Hello,' she said.

'Hello,' said Mark, surprised.

'Hello Keziah,' I said.

Everyone looked at everyone else.

'Er … do you want me to step out?' I asked. 'I need to … I need some highlighter pens.'

'Don't bother.'

'What if I need to highlight something—'

'Mark,' she said to the venture capitalist. 'Last night. Sorry. Sorry … I probably wouldn't mind if we did see more of each other. If … if that thought is still on the table.'

She blushed.

Keziah.

Blushed.

To the ears.  'Late for court bye.'

She turned stiffly and yanked a door handle. She was tired. It was the broom cupboard.

'You might want to try the other door,' I suggested. 'I think that's a cleaning cupboard.'

Keziah swore at me and was gone.

Mark looked at me.

'Did that just happen?'

'I think so,' I said.

'Huh,' said Mark.

'Maybe another cappuccino,' I said. 'Hope you know what you're doing.'

'Me too.'

# THE MERRY MONTH OF MAY

Nothing sorted itself out too well for the Oyster Cafe in the weeks that followed. Elspeth and her fellow trustees did sell to a developer, as they were now obliged to, with an uninsured, ruined building to clear before development could start.

Stub had a breakdown, as is normal after a few weeks' exertion, but Corrie and Jonah were easing him back to health.

Michael continued to open Madge's twice weekly. It did good as usual, but still seemed like an idea that had not quite got off the ground. Yet Michael seemed happy enough. He was always content these days and the clouds of sadness that used to hang around him had gone, which was surprising because outwardly nothing much had changed.

Mark and I started to get occupied with other clients.

Mark and Keziah were doing just fine. Amazing. There must have been some love software lodged inside Keziah's head all along. No-one would have guessed that it would run on the clunky operating system of her heart.

She seemed to develop new skills. Poking Mark, for example. Teasing him. Deflating him. Arguing passionately with him. Was she wearing different clothes or wearing the same clothes differently? Beats me. But she seemed to look a lot less dog-eared than she used to. She and I were still working together, and that experience for me had become a little less like tidying Queen Cleopatra's final fruit bowl.

I don't know if you'll ever hear about the adventures we were all having.

*

Spring came and soon enough the merry, chilly, hopeful, frustrating month of May, six months after the fire.

It was painful to see the site of the former Strict and Particular Baptist Chapel fenced off and a sign outside indicating that apartments were to be built. Nor were Elspeth and her fellow trustees able to donate money to the Oyster Cafe project, because, detached from a physical site, it didn't exist in a sufficiently clear legal form to be a legatee of the chapel's money.

Leopold, we heard, was offering consultancy and preparing a course on Successful Spiritual Conflict in an Age of Scepticism.

Everyone seem to be healing, though. Mark, Michael, Keziah. The project collapses and the souls grow. Interesting. Everyone healing, except me.

# ARMISTICE DAY

It wasn't a dream. Lottie was wearing a red below-the-knee woollen skirt, with dark tights and leather ankle-boots that I seemed to remember we bought together long ago. Up top was a flecked woollen roll-neck sweater, which is a good choice in my opinion when you are slender, or stick-thin, as is Lottie. Adds a bit of bulk. On top of that, belying Lottie's occasional penchant for the fashion adventure, was a cape and a beret.

Out of nowhere she had written to me.

She had written to me and it wasn't a dream.

We left her car and crunched along a gravelly, muddy, yellow path. To our left was a deep channel in which sailing boats were moored, whose rigging flicked and rang in the cruel wind. To our right were some scrubby sand-dunes, a beach, and the grey sea which was flecked with foam like it was dangerously mad. Seagulls patrolled it and called out warnings to us. I had my hands in the pockets of my bulky coat, and to my surprise, Lottie slipped her hand gently onto my arm.

If this was a cue to hold hands I decided to ignore it, for two reasons: (1) in case it wasn't and (2) because the wind was taking no prisoners and unlike Lottie, I wasn't wearing gloves.

'Bit of a walk first,' I said. 'Then we can enjoy a righteous thrill with our hot chocolate. All we'll be doing is putting back calories we just lost.'

We trod through the gravel.

'Sort of a Dickens landscape this,' I mused, trying some Librarian talk. 'Like the beginning of David Copperfield or something.'

'Arguably,' she said.

Not too many clues from that single word. And our drive here had been mostly silent. What was flashing about in that Senior Librarian's head, under that woolly beret? Were we still talking a frozen landscape of anger and grief? Was I still a hostile? But if so, why had she asked me here? Why the gentle resting of her hand on the arm? Does that mean anything or is it noise, rather than signal?

This was hopeless. To be honest, I need labelled items the size of builder's lumber when I'm trying to make sense of an emotional landscape. It'd be a miracle to get this right.

We crunched along in the blustery wind. The sea crashed and the pebbles clinked, unwillingly dragged back into the maw. The channel to our left became too narrow for boats and turned reedy, but still we could hear the ringing of the wind in the rigging behind us. This was bird-watching land, and avians were honking, whistling and tweeting with due application, not realising it was wasted on us.


*O you Censer, O you Golden Censer, slop, O slop on me.*
'Thank you for sending those chocolates and flowers,' she said.

'A pleasure,' I said.

I gulped. 'I wanted to get back what we lost. We both.'

'I don't,' said Lottie. 'What we lost wasn't worth having.'

I was hurt by this.

'I'd like to say I've changed. I haven't really,' I went on. 'Same old faults warmed over.'

'You didn't used to think you *had* faults.'

'True. But I've concluded after careful scrutiny it's just possible there are lingering elements of insensitivity and chauvinism in my own soul. Traces, you know. I might conceivably at times be a little annoying.'

I risked a look across at her face. The wind made her face look alive. She was looking down.

Eventually she said, 'I'm not in a place to do anything or be anything. I'm sorry. I'm really sorry.'

'That's all right.'

'So no more chocolates, thank you.'

'They've just started doing a salted chilli caramel with tabasco sauce,' I said. 'You've no idea. But: OK.'

She squeezed my arm briefly, and we walked on.

# THANKS

This is all made up and not based on anyone.

Many thanks to my beta readers who asked me questions of frightening complexity, such as, 'Wasn't Pascal a Jansenist'? Sarah Kasparian and Gareth Owens helped me with planning minutiae. Cy Winskell pointed out (among much else) where the Black Dog mispronounced things he'd pronounced correctly before. Andy Chamberlain, Gareth, Andrew Bowker, Helen Stedeford, Dan Cossette and others climbed into the book like proper editors, made so many helpful suggestions and assuaged the loneliness of solo composition. Insanely kind, all of you.

The soggy pudding of prose that's left, therefore, I have to take the blame for.

Sam Richardson wonderfully re-designed all the covers with illustrations by Simon Henshaw.

My wife and children give me what Jamie seeks and never finds, knowing me and loving me, both at the same time.

You can find my books and me on facebook and Twitter (@glenn_myers) and at glennmyers.info.

Keep in touch.

# ABOUT THE AUTHOR

Brought up in West Yorkshire, Glenn has lived in Los Angeles, Singapore, London and Cote d'Ivoire, but has settled with his wife in Cambridge, UK. They have two grown-up children.

Glenn has a bachelor's degree in physics and a MA in which was quite a bit of theology. Unlike the rest of his family, neither of his degrees is from Cambridge University and so he is considered a slow learner.

He enjoys cafes, curries, board games and his hammock.

To hear about new books, and see some behind-the-scenes stuff, go to glennmyers.info. He's also on Twitter at glenn_myers.